Issue 11
October–November 2018

Lezli Robyn & Tina Smith, Editors
Shahid Mahmud, Publisher

Published by Arc Manor/Heart's Nest Press
P.O. Box 10339
Rockville, MD 20849-0339

Heart's Kiss is published in February, April, June, August, October and December.

www.HeartsKiss.com

Pleaee refer to our website for information on how to submit material for *Heart's Kiss* magazine.

Available by subscription (www.HeartsKiss.com) or through your favorite online store (Amazon.com, BN.com, etc.).

ISBN: 978-1-61242-430-9

FOREIGN LANGUAGE RIGHTS: Please refer all inquiries pertaining to foreign language rights to Shahid Mahmud, Arc Manor, P.O. Box 10339, Rockville, MD 20849-0339. Tel: 1-240-645-2214. Fax 1-310-388-8440. Email admin@ArcManor.com.

Contents

OPENING EDITORIAL

by Tina Smith

It's hard to believe it's been nearly a year since Lezli and I started editing *Heart's Kiss* magazine. In the beginning we didn't know if this magazine would be around a year later or if readers would love short romance as much as we do, but we're still here and love hearing from fans of the magazine—looks like we've gotten many of you hooked as much as we are on our talented writers.

And this month is no different. We have the return of Gracie Wilson, with a new adult romance novella, *Beautifully Imagined*. To celebrate our foray into young love we've also included a special non-fiction article, *How Different Voices are Changing the YA Romance Landscape*, by newcomer Karen McCoy. Karen works as a librarian in California and has read the genre extensively to bring readers her recommendations as well as the latest tropes that are gaining popularity in YA. Going with our young love theme, a lot of our stories in this issue are sweeter in style. If you're thirsting for more recommended reads after Karen's article, be sure to flip to our back pages for C.S. DeAvilla's picks for this issue too.

We've also got another newcomer to welcome in to *Heart's Kiss*: Brenda Carre. Brenda has written an exciting supernatural suspense romance, *St. Jean and the Wish*, featuring a jinn who is holding on to one last wish to grant. Will that wish bring true love? We'll see.

Several writers this issue are returning to delight us with more tales of love. Juliet Marillier's *Far Horizons* shows us once again how much emotion can be conveyed with a short word count in her romance about finding love again, when older. Three more regulars have also returned, Olivette Devaux, has penned readers a new paranormal story, *The Forbidden Kiss of Life*, set in her native Czech Republic, and David Hendrickson is back as well with *From A Dry, Bitter Stream Comes the Sweetest of Fountains*, which is a great story about female empowerment in a time when women had no voice unless they met the right partner. Rei Rosenquist has written quite a treat this issue—a romance that includes non-binary characters. *The Heart Finds a Way* will sweep you into an alien world where every birthing pair has a third "hand." A third person in the relationship who cares for their pair in a way that makes them a complete family unit. But what happens when two hands fall in love? This world handles gender neutral pronouns in a beautiful way. In the English language we refer to "he/him" and "she/her," but there are many who do not identify as either male or female, so Rei introduces the gender-neutral pronouns of "ze/zer" in their story. While gender neutral pronouns are not a new thing—the practice going back centuries, being used in not only the foundations of our language system in English, but also in many other languages and cultures around the world—we are delighted that *The Heart Finds a Way* will be our first story to use them in *Heart's Kiss*.

It's not just fiction authors we're excited to announce, but a new column featuring romance-themed recipes by Andrea Abedi, chef extraordinaire: The Temptress Presents. We cannot wait to see what delicious meal she cooks up for our seasonal-themed issues. The interviews in this issue feature bestseller and by-popular-request, Brenda Jackson. A little birdie tells me (Okay—it is Lezli!) that both her and Susan Donovan are working exclusive novellas for us, to appear in our Christmas and Valentines issues. Squee!

Do you love beta heroes? I do. This issue's *You Read That?* column, by Julie Pitzel, is going to dive deep into the hero archetype of betas, why they're misunderstood, and why they make great protagonist material. In a related note, Julie has been keeping a huge secret from us: she writes amazing poetry! *Wedding Night* not only tells a wonderful story about the most intimate part of couple's nuptial day, but it has beat and rhyme that had Lezli and I swooning at the end.

Lezli and I had a blast this year at the Romance Writers of America national conference in Denver, getting to meet so many of our featured (and future) authors as well as industry professionals. Some of those pictures of our adventures are included in this issue. We were warmed with how well-received *Heart's Kiss* has been in the industry and at the conference, and we plan to continue to find writers you love, from the popular and soon-to-be popular, to continue to bring you the stories that make you sigh. Our goals and dreams are growing with your enthusiasm. Thank you for reading and please enjoy the latest issue of *Heart's Kiss*.

Brenda Jackson is an American novelist who writes contemporary multicultural romance novels. She was the first African-American author to have a novel published as part of the Silhouette Desire line and has seen many of her novels reach the New York Times *and* USA Today *bestsellers lists. Brenda reached a milestone in her career in October, 2013 when she published her 100ᵗʰ novel, becoming the first African-American to achieve such an accomplishment. Brenda has received many awards and accomplishments. She was the first African-American romance author to make* USA Today's *Bestsellers List and to make the* New York Times *bestsellers List. Brenda is the recipient of the RWA Nora Roberts Lifetime Achievement Award 2012, the highest honor bestowed by RWA in recognition of significant contributions to the romance genre. Additionally, she received the Sara Blocker Award 2012 from Florida Memorial University, the highest award given to a female for exceptional service to the university and for community service. In 2012 she also became the NAACP Image Award Nominee for Outstanding Literary Fiction for her novel,* A Silken Thread.

HEART'S KISS INTERVIEWS BRENDA JACKSON

by Lezli Robyn

It was my pleasure to sit down with Brenda Jackson at the Romance Writers of America Conference in Denver, Colorado, this past July. Not only was she warm and insightful, but also very educational on what it is like to grow up in a country that didn't always celebrate diversity. Her answers about her career, and how much the love of her life influenced her writing, gives me no doubt as to why she's so celebrated today.

Lezli Robyn: I would like to say first, thank you for doing this interview for our magazine. I know you must be incredibly busy this RWA.

Brenda Jackson: Oh, you're welcome!

LR: We actually had people commenting on our Facebook page, asking us when we will get Brenda Jackson in our issues, and I was like "You might see

her appear in our pages soon," knowing we were having an interview here! *laughs*

BJ: *laughs* Ohhh, that is so lovely! I'm touched. *flicking through copies of our magazine* Wow, I love it.

LR: Thank you. We wanted to go all out for our print issues. We love the silhouettes of women and couples we get to place after individual content in our magazine. You don't get to see them in the ebook version.

BJ: Yeah, I like the print copy. At lot of times, when I'm traveling, I just like to have a print copy to put on my coffee table and places like that.

What type of fiction do you look for in your magazine?

LR: All forms of romance. We publish original fiction, and reprints too. We can also serialize. So if you, for example, only had long-length pieces, we can print them over several issues. If it's a reprint, we print them with no exclusivity—you can publish it elsewhere at the same time. If it's new fiction, the authors like us because we only ask for two months exclusivity—that's it.

BJ: Oh, that is wonderful. So what size stories do you need?

LR: With our format we can do pretty much any length. If you came to us and said you had a forty-thousand-word piece, we can split it over two issues. Twenty-five-thousand or less, we can put it in one issue as our featured novella. Susan Donovan is actually doing one for us now, for our Christmas issue.

BJ: Oh, wow.

I will have to think about a Valentine's story. Have you got anyone to do a Valentine's novella?

LR: No, we don't. We would *love* to buy a Valentine's piece from you!

discusses logistics; editor inwardly happy dances

So now I will ask you some questions! Let's ask the most obvious one first: How did you get into writing?

BJ: Well, I started entertaining my classmates. It's funny that the issue now is diversity. That has *always* been an issue. Keep in mind, I am sixty-five, so I grew up in America during the era of segregation.

LR: That is terrible. I still can't quite imagine it, although I know Australia has also had its shady past with segregating the first nation of our country.

BJ: I remember, as a little girl, going to a color-only bathroom. I remember going downtown with my mom, saying: "Let's go to this store!" And she said: "We're not allowed in that store." I remember that period of time vividly.

So, when I started storytelling in the eighth grade there were no books about people that looked like me, or my classmates. So you read and you watch what you have available. I would watch these shows and then write those type of stories for my classmates, as a thirteen-year-old—they were sweet romances. But I would convert the stories so that they were about people that looked like me, spending a summer on the beach. There was only one African-American beach in my area, so you had to go to that beach.

LR: Really? So even a beach was segregated?

BJ: *Anywhere.* We had our own beach, which became a landmark. If we wanted to go to the beach, that was the only one we could go to.

So I wrote stories of this boy and girl who met at the beach, and every so often, while I was on the beach over the summer, I would add more stories about them getting to know each other.

I wrote on notebook paper, and then when school started in the fall, I had a lot of things written down, so I would entertain my classmates with these stories, passing them around school. We did not have typing machines, so I had to write ten sets of the same story. As a result, my classmates always thought I should be an author. But I had done it as a way to entertain myself.

LR: And to imagine a better world.

BJ: Right.

My class at high school was the last all Black class. So I didn't even go to school with any white kids at all. None.

LR: That is amazing (and not in a good way).

BJ: I am blessed. When I started working at State Farm Insurance Company, while I was going to college, that is when I first encountered my association with whites. There were some that acted like I thought they would act. But then there were some who befriended me.

LR: Like me.

BJ: Yes, exactly.

My friend and I, we would go on break together, and we found out things like the fact that when you perm your hair, it's to make it curly, but when I perm my hair it's to make it straight. *laughs*

LR: That is hilarious. There is the contrast, but also the similarity in actions.

BJ: Yes, so we learned from each other. And we found out that the only difference was this. *points towards her skin* She was like: "I'm going to try and get as dark as you. As soon as summer comes, I'm gonna go get my tan on! *laughs*

LR: So what happened next?

BJ: I got married out of high school. I met my childhood sweetheart and went to college and in my company—State Farms—I moved up the corporate ladder until I was in management. And so obviously I didn't think about writing; I was busy. But when I went to my school reunion, my classmates (remembering I was always writing, back when they knew me) would ask: "Did you ever write a book?"

"No, I'm Miss Corporate America."

They said: "No, your true calling is writing."

LR: Oh, wow. So how old were you at this point, to get perspective?

BJ: I was twenty-eight when I went to my ten-year class reunion, because I was eighteen when I graduated. Ten years later, at thirty-eight, they were asking again where the book was. And my husband told me: "Before you go to another class reunion, you have to write that book."

LR: *laughs*

BJ: I was like: "I don't even know if I *can* write one. So my husband said: "Find out what you need to do." So that was when I started coming to RWA. My husband bought me my first ticket.

LR: Your husband sounds like a real sweetheart.

BJ: Oh, he was a sweetheart. He died four years ago. We had been married forty-two years. I still wear the going-steady ring he gave me.

LR: I was given my folks going-steady ring on my sixteenth birthday, when Mom no longer could wear it.

BJ: I won't ever take mine off! I've been wearing it since I was fifteen. It was on this hand *points to left hand* until he put my engagement ring on, and then I moved it to my other hand and it hasn't moved since.

So, anyway, I came to RWA, and the first year, I had to admit, I was a groupie. I saw Jayne Ann Krentz, Julie Garwood—all of them—and I was like: "Can I have you autograph?"

When I got back, my husband was like: "So, what did you learn?" And I was like: "Welllll...I need to go back next year to learn."

So then I started going to the workshops, taking notes. And then I would start making notes. And so, what they do at RWA is give you free books, and I started reading the books. I would travel a lot with my job, and so I would read them in the hotel rooms in the evening. Sometimes I would say:

"I can't believe someone would buy this." Others I would read and go: "Wow. This is wonderful."

I would report back to my husband and say what I would like about some books and what I think I could do better about others. And he said: "Then do it. If you think you can do better, then *what* would you do better?"

There were some books that would have the wrong ending—they needed a HEA [happily-ever-after]. I believed in a HEA because I was a HEA. I could see my husband and I living not only to death do us part, but even after death. Which I am doing now, because I am still so madly in love with this man, as if he was still alive.

LR: He is your person.

BJ: Yes. That is why I still wear my rings. Me and my husband talked about it, because he died of cancer. He knew to not even suggest to me that I meet someone else, because I knew in my heart, I got his rib. I really believe that. And since I have his rib, I don't need nobody else's rib.

I had to explain it to guys, who approached me, who know my husband died, asking me: "Why are you still wearing his rings when he has been gone now for four years?" I was like: "And?"

LR: You didn't divorce, did you? You are still married.

BJ: Yes, exactly! And I'm like: "Why does that matter?" And he said: "Because he would want you to be happy." I told him he did not know my husband. My husband knew my happiness was with him. So he made sure I knew how to make it by myself, after he was gone, because he knew I would be by myself.

LR: Your husband was not wanting you *not* to find love. He just knew that he *was* your only love.

BJ: That is right. You understand. He left me financially able, so I could still enjoy the things in my life I still love to do, even without him. I read for him, because when I'm lonely, I'm lonely for him. But I *am* happy. I was just happiest with him.

So anyway, my husband said: "Write the book." So I wrote one book, and I had so much fun that I wrote another one, and then it became a series before I sold it. When I finally sold it to an imprint of Kensington, I tried to sell them all three. And they said: "Let us do one, and we'll see how it works."

They didn't have to wait on me to write another one. As soon as that one started to sell I said: "Here you go!" *laughs* I was always ahead of the game. I was always three or so books ahead, even with my full-time job.

LR: When did you have time to write?

BJ: I didn't do it at work. I did it at home, or while I was sitting in the bleachers at my kid's little league game. When everyone clapped I knew to look up and clap and be a good mom.

At the time there was no computers, so I always wrote longhand. And then I went home and I would type everything onto my typewriter—my husband bought my first one. But, basically, that is how I started.

LR: That is a wonderful story. It seems that what you're saying is your career started off as a couple. Your husband was in every aspect of your career.

BJ: Right. When I write I try to convey in every one of my heroes a part of him.

LR: That's beautiful. He was your example of a perfect man.

BJ: I would tell people: "My mother died when I was eighteen. My grandmother died when I was forty. I was with my husband, when he died, for forty-seven years. Longer than I had been with my mother or my grandmother. So we grew up together. He taught me a lot about life. He taught me a lot about love, passion. All of it I attribute to him."

So when my sons said I'm acting like Daddy now—you know, when I put my hand down and say: "No. You can't have that. That is not how it's going to work." Well, they're grown men, and they say it is like Daddy's still here when I do that. And I tell them I have to act like that because your daddy is not here now, but we were always a team.

LR: They are seeing the partnership still.

BJ: Right. And they appreciate that.

LR: Which book do you think pinpointed the time where you suddenly knew you had a successful writing career?

BJ: I think *One Special Moment*. That is the book that won RT's Best Multicultural Book of the Year Reviewers' Choice Award. And then Walden Books gave my sixth book, *Fire and Desire*, an award. And I was like: "Wow!" That is when I was recognized that I was getting noticed.

But still, I would tell people, this is just what I do on the side. I am Miss Corporate America. I knew where my check was coming in from every two weeks, so this was to help us get extra money, to put towards a repair bill or college fund. It would also allow me to go to all the conferences I wanted to and buy the clothes I wanted to to look the part at work or play. So that is what that novel money helped me to do, but it was never going to be my career.

LR: The Insurance career was your stable job.

BJ: Yes. My career was to work up the corporate ladder.

LR: It makes sense. You never quite know if you are going to make it in the writing field, and keep making it. You do a lot of work, even before you get paid. Especially starting out.

BJ: It all depends on your readers. Whether there are readers to buy your book, and whether they are invested enough to buy your next book. And I didn't want to depend on that. That is why I never quit my day job. I kept moving up with the company, but I used writing to keep me sane. I was studying so much about insurance, taking all these exams to get different insurance licenses, so when I needed to clear my mind, I would pull out a romance novel from my purse, or I would write. That is how I would escape.

LR: When did you start to write full-time?

BJ: It was only when I was with the company thirty-something years, and had written fifty-some books while working—books that made *New York Times* lists—that I changes happened in my life.

I really did not want to leave. I was the one that said that if I won the lotto, I'm still going to work. I loved my job. I loved bringing people in, doing what I did. I loved being Miss Corporate America, being in charge. I just loved representing my company.

My company really helped, because they said: "Oh, we've got this celebrity person working for us. And we are trying to expand into diversity. She would be the best person to send to represent the company, at book signings and whatever, to show we are a diverse company."

And that is what they did. I had the best of both words. So why should I quit?

LR: And if you can do both, and you were passionate about both jobs in your life…

BJ: I was happy. And then Harlequin came and said: "We'll make you an offer you can't refuse." And I was like: "It's gotta be a darn good offer, because I like what I do. My boss will tell you I run the company."

They made me an offer. And they said: "Not only will you get a chance to come home and retire, and write full-time, but your husband can, too."

I knew that while I might have loved my job, he was getting frustrated with his. He had worked there a long time, and it was shift work, in a manufacturing type plant. If I took this offer, I could bring him home. Then we could get together and work as a team, and I owed him that for supporting me all these years.

LR: That is wonderful.

BJ: Well, then both our boys said: "We want to go to Ivy League schools." I knew that was going to cost money. So I realized I need to write more books, but it was a decision we made together.

We both retired, then. However, we decided he will retire a year before me, because he was two years older than me. So I told him: "You come home, enjoy yourself, do what you want to do, until I come home with the Honey Do list in a year."

LR: I love that. *laughs*

BJ: So when I came home, I started my own publishing company. It was to publish books I wrote where readers would ask: "What about the uncle? I would love to read his story." It was so I could publish characters in the age group that were older.

If you go by Harlequin's guidelines, the hero had to be thirty-something and younger. They didn't want stories about the father or the older uncle, because that was not their demographic. So I told them: "I need to write about the people you don't usually want me to write about, when I'm not writing for you." Now, granted, they're publishing stories about the full-figured woman now, and times are changing. But at the time, I created the company to write about the rejects.

LR: Or, you know, the other ninety percent of the population. *laughs*

BJ: Exactly. *laughs*

Women would write me and say: "Look, I'm eighty years old, and reading about your thirty-year-old hero is like reading about what my grandson would be doing. I don't want to know what he is doing!"

LR: So she was thinking that she would like to be fifty again, and so she would *love* to hear about fifty-year-olds.

BJ: Yes! Or another would ask: "My husband passed away after we raised our children, and I want to believe there is a second chance at love. Would you write about this?"

So that is what I decided to do. Instead of writing new people for my imprint. I would look at the people I had already written about and write about their older relatives.

LR: Now I had watched your movie, before I knew it was your movie. *Truly Everlasting.* I did not know it was based on your book.

BJ: My son directed it.

LR: Oh, really?!

BJ: What happened is, my son graduated from college. You see, *leans in confidentially* they thought I was writing to educate them, because they went to Ivy League colleges. One went to Columbia and the other went to Cornell. I would tell them the same thing my momma would: "Do you all think money grows on trees?" And they would say: "Just write another book, Mom." That was stuff my younger son would say, coz he thought I was writing for just their wants and desires. *laughs*

So what actually happened is my son, he was moving to California. He had gotten his Bachelors in Columbia, then got his Masters in Film, and he wanted our support to help him get set up in California. I had already put eight years into this kid's learning, but I didn't know what he could do. So my husband said: "You got all those books back there. Let him make one of those into a movie." He said it like it was no big deal. *laughs*

I told him: "It costs money to make a film." He said: "Well, take it out of my 401K. As long as you give it back. I believe in your skills as a business woman to know how to run a business. So set him up. You and I will be the executive producers, and he will direct it and hire his staff, and it will educate him. Plus, it will let us know what he can do."

I was like: "Oh, okay. How much money are we talking about here, because I have never looked at your 401k, but I do know movies cost money." His response was: "I'm willing to give him half a million dollars." I was like: "Whaaat?!?" I didn't know he had that kind of money.

LR: *laughs* This is gold—literally.

BJ: He had built himself an empire, after thirty years of contributions, and them matching it. But, he said, understandably: "I have to get my money back, for retirement."

So that is what we did. We loaned my son the money. We basically hired a lot of talented people from different film schools around the country. We bought two houses to film in, because I was on a budget. If you paid cash for the houses, you could get them reasonably cheap, and my husband was happy with what I was doing, because I had to sign off on everything.

We were not selling to the big screen; the movie was going straight to DVD, so I needed to find out how many DVDs we needed to sell to give my husband his money back. So I knew, that in order to give him back his money, after expenses were costed out, I had to make the DVD twenty-five dollars each. And I explained that to my husband.

He was like: "Brenda, who the hell is going to want to pay twenty-five for a DVD when Avatar"—he thought Avatar was the best movie ever—"only cost me nineteen ninety-nine, and I cried paying nineteen ninety-nine."

LR: *laughs*

BJ: I said: "My readers will." Because they believed in me.

LR: To them, it is like buying a hardcover book of yours.

BJ: Exactly. I owed them this.

And so he said: "You know your readers."

I put the finished DVD out around the holidays. My readers were not just buying one, they were buying four or five copies, to give some to their families for Christmas. My husband could not believe it.

The movie sold so well, it got the attention of different movie labels—like the head for Warner Brothers. He came to me, and I said: "Well, I don't really need y'all. I'm already selling them. I've got this covered."

LR: *laughs* This is amazing.

BJ: My son was like: "Mom, this is a big deal. They could put it in Walmart. They could—"

Well, let me tell you what my response was: "Let me wait until I get your father's money back. Then, whether or not we sell it after that, I at least have his money covered."

And so that is what happened. Then Netflix picked it up for three years.

LR: That is where I watched it!

BJ: Then it was on Amazon. Now, basically you can just buy it as the DVD; I'm selling it directly.

And so that is how the movie came about. We ended up making interest! Then we started a foundation, to give college students part of the profit.

LR: This is great. That was going to be my next question!

BJ: My foundation was established for my grandmother, because she was a southern lady, a Baptist lady. She used to make pies and tea cakes, to send money to this college in Florida, called the Memorial University. That was a Baptist-owned college for African-American students. Now anyone can go there, but back in the day we couldn't go to any college, so the Baptist church started this college.

She was a strong woman that sent money all the time. And I loved my grandma so much, I said that if I ever make money doing anything, I would start a scholarship in her name.

LR: That is lovely.

BJ: So even before we started the movie, I would give them around fifteen thousand a year. And then when the movie went so big, and we had a movie premiere, I called the college. They came to the movie premiere and I presented them with a check, and I have presented them with big checks ever since.

Now I do my cruise, every two years and I have four scholarships I hand out. So that is what we do.

LR: So what is new for you?

BJ: I'm working on a new movie. I have a three-book contract with this company, and I think my book is next on their list to go into filming. I have so many books. I'm working with author Iris Bolling, too, who just turned Bev's book into a movie.

LR: Yes, Beverly Jenkin's book, *Deadly/Sexy*.

BJ: Iris will be looking to do my book next. I don't have the half a million to give her that my husband gave me, since that is the money my husband now gave me, in his death, to live off for the rest of my life. But we're doing a fundraiser on GoFundMe and whatever we can do to raise money!

I'm also introducing a new series, in late October, which it is location based, coming out from Harlequin. The first book is one hundred and twenty thousand words. It was supposed to be ninety thousand words, but I couldn't end the book, it was such an intense story. Stay tuned for more details about that one!

LR: Thank you so very much for the interview. This has been lovely!

BJ: I have loved it. I need to know where to buy your magazines…

*shows Brenda our *Heart's Kiss* website*

Copyright © 2018 by Lezli Robyn.

AT LONG
LAST

NEW YORK TIMES BESTSELLING AUTHOR

BRENDA JACKSON

excerpt from
AT LONG LAST

by Brenda Jackson

Release Date: October 9, 2018

Tampa, Florida
LOGAN

> *"Yesterday is not ours to recover, but tomorrow is ours to win or lose."*
>
> —Lyndon B. Johnson

"Are you watching the news, Logan?"

Logan Montgomery had just entered his condo after having spent a day out on the bay with friends. He paused at the sound of panic in his brother Lance's voice. Lance never got worked up about anything…except for that time a few years ago, when he thought he'd lost Asia, the woman he loved. "No, I'm just walking in the door. I was out on the boat all day. Why?"

"There was a bombing in a restaurant in Algiers."

Logan felt the blood drain from his face at the same time his heart began pounding painfully in his chest. "Claire?" he said, in a voice wrenched with sudden fear. When Lance didn't answer quick enough, he said, "Dammit, Lance, has Asia heard from Claire?" Moving quickly, he walked through his kitchen and grabbed the remote off the table, then clicked on the television in the family room.

Claire was Asia's older sister and the woman Logan hoped to marry one day, although Claire didn't have a clue. They had met through their individual siblings a few years ago and that first time had been enough for Logan to decide she was the woman he wanted to one day share his life with.

"No, Asia hasn't heard anything, and that has us worried. We tried calling but couldn't get through. Asia is on the phone in the other room with the State Department, but they don't have any information yet either."

Logan momentarily tuned out Lance's words to hear what the news reporter was saying on the television screen. The Shelton House in Algiers had been a popular eating place that catered to a huge crowd on the weekends. It was believed there had been just over sixty persons dining at the restaurant and it had been confirmed there were sixty dead. The bomb had been meant to blow up the entire restaurant and it had not only done that, but had destroyed a parking garage next door which had caused a major fire.

"Claire isn't someone who dines out a lot, so there's no reason to think she was there," Logan said, trying to reassure Lance as well as himself. He knew that much about Claire from their many talks. He would call her from time to time to see how she was doing.

"Usually she doesn't, but…"

"But what?" Logan asked, hearing the hesitation in his brother's voice. And it was enough to make his nerves go on edge.

"Asia talked with Claire earlier today. One of her friends had a birthday and they were getting together to celebrate at that particular restaurant…tonight. They had reservations for eight o'clock."

Logan knew there was a five-hour time difference between where he was in Tampa and Algiers. That meant Claire could have been there at the time of the bombing. His pounding heart suddenly froze. No! He refused to even consider it.

"Logan?"

"Yes?"

"I'll let you know when we hear something. Asia's been talking to her mother when she's not on the phone with the State Department."

"How is Ms. Annie holding up?" Logan asked. He had met Asia and Claire's mother at Lance's wedding and had liked her immediately.

"It's the not knowing that's driving everyone crazy. But don't worry. As soon as I hear anything, I'll let you know."

"Okay. Give Asia and the baby a kiss for me."

The moment he disconnected the call with Lance, Logan rubbed a hand down his face before moving toward the kitchen to grab a beer out the refrigerator. When his phone rang again, he quickly answered it. "Hello?"

"I guess you heard about the bombing in Algiers."

It was his brother Lyle. "Yes, Lance just called." He then relayed what Lance had told him about Asia talking to Claire earlier and her plans to go to that restaurant for dinner with friends.

"Let's hope she changed her mind or hadn't arrived yet," Lyle said softly.

"Yes, let's hope." He wasn't sure how he would handle it if that wasn't the case. In that instant, he suddenly felt much older than his forty years.

Logan ended the call with Lyle, and before he could finish his beer, his phone rang again. In the next few minutes, he got calls from his father, Jeremiah, and sister, Carrie, who both lived in Gary, Indiana. They too, had heard about the bombing and were hopeful Claire was safe.

After he finally managed to get off the phone, he headed for his patio that overlooked the bay. Dusk had settled in and as he dropped into a chair, he suddenly realized how many members of his family knew the way he felt about Claire. Yet, Claire, herself, didn't have the slightest idea.

He was certain at some point, she had picked up on the attraction between them, the sexual chemistry. It had been too strong for her not to have noticed. But they hadn't made any effort to act on it, and instead, had done their best to ignore it. At least she had. He couldn't. Because he'd known her career goals and her plans not to return to the United States to live on a permanent basis for at least a couple more years, he had been content to wait for her.

For one thing, he wasn't cut out for a long-distance relationship, which was all she could have offered him. If she was interested, at all.

Besides, if he was honest with himself, he'd have to admit he was enjoying his freedom. This was the first time in ten years that he didn't have to worry about anyone but himself. When she'd been eighteen, Carrie had moved in with him and had remained for eight years. Even while attending the local university, she had preferred living at home instead of in the dormitory or an apartment. The arrangement had suited them both fine. Carrie had needed him to extend his oldest brother role and he hadn't been in any hurry to relinquish it. Now Carrie was happily married to Connor and living in Gary near their father, and she and Connor were expecting their first baby.

He thought about his younger brothers, Lyle and Lance. Like him, Lyle had chosen a career in medicine. Logan, himself, was a plastic surgeon, while Lyle, who lived in Texas with his wife Monique, was a heart specialist. Lance, though, had taken a different path. He was a relationship guru and bestselling author. One of his novels, The Playa's Handbook, which supposedly perfected the art of being a single man, namely a playa, had caused quite a national stir a few years back. Now the die-hard player was happily married with a seven-month-old son named Leland.

Logan stretched his legs out in front of him. This had been an eventful year. Leland had been born in February, Lyle had gotten married in April and Carrie's baby was due in the spring. Everyone seemed to be moving on. Everyone but him.

He took another sip of his beer, remembering the first time he'd met Claire Fowler. It was after Lance and Asia's turbulent love affair which finally ended in marriage. Logan and Claire had met at the rehearsal dinner on Paradise, the island where the wedding had taken place.

In a way, he'd known before meeting Claire that he would like her, mainly because she had been instrumental in helping Lance win over Asia. He'd figured if a woman like Asia could blow the mind of a die-hard bachelor like Lance Montgomery, she must be one hell of a woman. And if Claire was anything like her sister, then meeting her would be worth his time and effort. It had been.

As he sat there, watching the sun set, he could recall the night they'd met, just as if it had been yesterday…

Logan walked alongside Lyle, as they made their way to the courtyard where the others were waiting to start the rehearsal for Lance's wedding. It wouldn't be a large ceremony, since Lance and Asia had opted to invite just close friends and family. However, the wedding was attracting a lot of attention from the media because both Lance and Asia were renowned in the field of relationship expertise—but on opposite ends of the spectrum. News of their engagement gave hope to single women all over the country, and had the playas running for cover. Still, Logan was glad his brother had come to his senses before it was too late, and that Asia had forgiven Lance for past transgressions.

The minute Logan and Lyle rounded the corner, Logan caught a glimpse of the woman standing with Asia. Seeing the similarities in their features, Logan had no doubt that this was her sister Claire. As if she felt him staring, she glanced his way, their eyes connected and she smiled at him.

Logan walked over, with Lyle quietly following to where the two women stood with their brother, Lance. Asia quickly made introductions and the moment he'd taken Claire's hand in his, he'd known she was the one for him. Claire Fowler had not only caught his attention but just that quickly, she'd captured his heart.

Since Claire had been Asia's maid of honor, and Logan was to escort one of the bridesmaids, a friend of Asia's from college, during the rehearsal, it had been only later, after the huge barbeque, that he'd finally been able to speak with Claire again. It hadn't been hard to talk her into taking a walk on the beach with him.

"This is a beautiful island," she'd said as they walked along the shore.

"It is. Now I wish I would have bought it that time Lance had thought of selling. Of course, that was before he got Asia out here and they fell in love with it, and each other."

She chuckled and the soft sound carried with the wind. "Oh, I believe they were in love well before then. All they needed was a little push. Especially Asia. I am so happy for them."

Logan recalled that time. "You should be. You played a major part in bringing them together."

She didn't say anything for a moment as she looked out over the ocean. "I did what I felt I had to do." She shook her head. "Don't get me wrong, Sean is a really nice guy, but he was still David's brother. Eventually, David would have destroyed things between them. He's such an ass."

"So, I've heard."

"I couldn't let that happen. It took me only a short while to see that Asia's heart was with Lance. He makes her happy."

He nodded as he took a sip of his beer. "So, tell me, Claire, what makes you happy?"

She smiled and when she did, the dimples in both cheeks took his breath away. "My work makes me happy. I love what I do, working for the State Department. It was always my dream to travel and I'm doing just that. I never live in the same place for more than two years."

"What exactly do you do?"

"As a foreign service diplomat, I work closely with the Department of Defense as an educational consultant. My job is to make sure that the kids of our military men and women are getting a good education while they are living abroad with their parents who serve our country."

"I understand you went to Harvard."

"Yes, all the way through—I got my bachelors, masters and PhD. I understand you went there, as well."

He figured she'd heard that from Lance or Asia. "Yes, but I'm sure I'd finished before you got there. You're thirty, right?"

"Yes."

"I'm thirty-seven. So, we couldn't have been there at the same time."

"There are two years difference between you and Lyle, and four years between you and Lance, right?"

"Yes. Carrie came much later."

He figured she knew all the dysfunctional details of the Montgomery family, thanks to his mother.

"And where do you go next?" he asked, thinking again of how beautiful she was.

"After this year, I'm due to spend some time in Algiers. I've heard it's an incredible place—full of culture and history. I'm really looking forward to it."

"How long do you plan to do this job? You're so seldom home."

She shrugged. "I'm not sure. Probably just another couple of years. After tomorrow Asia will be married,

and I anticipate getting some nieces or nephews soon. As well, my mom is getting older, and I want to be around to spend more time with her. I haven't told Mom or Asia but after my assignment in Algiers, I'm thinking of taking a special assignment that would allow me to travel the way I like, only not as frequently. And my home base would be DC."

Logan nodded. She recognized that her mother was getting older. Newsflash. Her mother wasn't the only one. They were as well. Evidently, she wasn't one of those women who worried about getting married before a certain age. But then, neither was he one of those men. "Are you seeing anyone?"

She threw her head back and laughed. "Heck no. No man in his right mind would want to hook up with me now."

Was she giving him a hint? "Why do you say that?"

"Because I'm married to my job and I like it that way. I'm too busy to take on a man who wants any part of my time. And since I don't believe in long-distance affairs, what I have are male friends who have a clear understanding we are nothing more than friends."

He nodded. "I see." And he did. He had no problem giving her breathing room, because now that Lance and Carrie were married off, he could sure use some himself. He figured it wouldn't be long before the right woman came along for Lyle, too.

Waiting a couple of years for Claire to return to the States permanently wouldn't be so bad. He would be close to forty by then. He'd never figured he would marry before his fortieth birthday anyway, so her timeline might just work out with his.

"Mind if I call you now and then, to see how you're doing?" he asked her.

She smiled over at him. "No, I don't mind. Asia told me about your big brother complex."

His big brother complex? "And what did she tell you?"

"That you like looking out for people."

Yes, he couldn't resist doing that. After all, he'd had years of experience. But he did not have any big brother feelings when it came to her. There was nothing brotherly about what she did to him…

Logan's thoughts slowly returned to the present. He took the last sip from his beer, remembering. When he and Claire had parted ways two days after the wedding, he'd known Claire was the only woman for him. Since then, they'd spent time together whenever she'd returned to the States to attend family functions, and he made it a point to call her regularly to see how she was doing. Unfortunately, he was pretty sure she didn't suspect how he felt about her and had conveniently slotted him into that "male friends only" category. When he'd seen her four months ago at Lyle's wedding, he'd finally given in and kissed her, although it was only a brief brush of his lips on her forehead. But every time he saw her, it only reinforced his belief that one day they would be together.

Logan almost jumped out his skin when his phone rang. He glanced at the call display—it was Lance. His gut tightened as he clicked on the phone. "Yes, Lance?"

"Good news and bad news. The good news is that Claire finally got through and called to let us know she's safe. She wasn't feeling well, so she'd decided not to go. The bad news is that four of her friends were killed. If she'd been feeling better, things would have gone another way."

Logan knew what way Lance meant. "I'm just so relieved she's okay, although I'm very sorry about what happened to her friends."

"Something else you might be glad to hear is that she's coming home for a while. This incident has shaken her up pretty badly, Logan. Asia said she sounded grief-stricken."

"I can understand that. Will she be flying to Paradise?" Although Lance and Asia owned a beautiful home in Chicago, they had created the Montgomery Marriage Institute on Paradise Island. The institute specialized in working with couples in crisis by holding marriage seminars to help couples build, repair, and strengthen their marriages.

"Asia asked her to come here, but Claire wants to spend a couple of weeks at her place in DC. She said she needs some time to get a handle on a few things…alone. She was pretty adamant about that."

Logan nodded. Luckily, she hadn't made the same request of him. She needed him, whether she knew it or not. Right now, she only saw him as Asia's brother-in-law. However, that was about to change.

"This might be a good time to read my latest book—How to Jumpstart a Lasting Relationship. It might give you a few pointers when you see her."

Logan lifted a brow. God, his brother knew him well. "What makes you think I'll see her?"

"Hey, let's not get cute, Logan. And speaking of books, I can read you like one. You're going to see her."

Lance was right. He was going to see her. Everyone who mattered to him knew he was in love with Claire Fowler. Now it was time that she knew it as well.

Juliet Marillier is a multi Aurealis, Tin Duck, and Sir Julius Vogel Award winner and recipient of the Le Prix Imaginales for her historical fantasy fiction. Her novels are published simultaneously by major publishers in United States and Australia and are translated into other languages all around the world. Known for combining folkloric fantasy with historical fiction, her novels are often filled with sensitive depictions of the transformative journey a person can go through, metaphorically and physically, to protect their family and future partner—even characters who once thought themselves too broken or incapable of love. Born in New Zealand, Juliet now resides in Western Australia with a delightful menagerie of elderly dogs.

FAR HORIZONS

by Juliet Marillier

The novels were doing well. *Dawn* had covered Kate's uni fees, *Goddess* had paid the deposit on Sean's flat and *Whisper* had helped set Bella up in her graphic design business. My publisher had just offered me a new three-book contract.

The children took me out to lunch to celebrate. Over the second bottle of chardonnay they went serious.

"Mum," declared Kate, "it's time you spent some money on *yourself*."

"I do," I protested. "I've just had the gutters and down-pipes replaced."

"Oh, Mum," sighed Bella, "you know what we mean. A smart hairdo, a pair of killer shoes, something for *you*."

"A wolfhound," suggested Sean. "A harpsichord. Riding lessons."

"I might *like* those things, but I don't *need* them."

Finances had always been tight after the divorce, with no extra for school trips or designer labels. We'd managed, the four of us, thanks to good management and our shared sense of humour. I'd been amazed and grateful—still was—that my new career as a romance novelist had made me, if not filthy rich, at least comfortably well off.

"Get the hairdo anyway," said Bella. "You're starting to look grandmotherly, Mum. Here, I've got a discount coupon for Ennio's. They've pencilled you in for two-thirty."

Ennio gave me a severely stylish cut and softened my natural silvery grey with subtle highlights. Looking in the mirror I felt an odd sensation, as if I were a balloon about to float away on an adventure all its own.

Walking to the bus, I spotted a poster of pale minarets against a dusky sky, and another beside it of a teeming market full of brassware and vivid carpets. The name of the shop was Far Horizons.

"Nothing venture, nothing win," I muttered, stepping inside and taking a numbered ticket. There were lots of people waiting: three girls in low-slung jeans; a white-haired man calmly reading a book; older couples armed with maps and travel guides. I was dying for a coffee.

I leafed through the books and magazines. *Boomers A Looming Burden on Health System*, screamed the Bulletin. I put it down and picked up the daily paper. *SKIN: Spoiled and Selfish*, the headline read. Scanning the piece, I learned that SKIN stood for "Spend the Kids' Inheritance Now."

The queue progressed as sales staff called customers in turn. It was clear Far Horizons preferred to employ attractive people in their twenties, in keeping with their specialty: adventure travel. Their brochures featured athletic, glowing young things, and the staff matched. Perhaps I'd make it to the desk to discover I was too old and selfish to travel as far as Geraldton, let alone Turkey.

I flipped through a gossip mag. *Sixty is the New Twenty* was blazoned over pictures of ageing celebrities, nipped and tucked and botoxed into weird approximations of their younger selves. On the next page, I read *Boomers Monopolise the Holiday Market*. I sighed. Maybe I should be spending my money on a tea cosy or a pair of fluffy slippers.

"They say we baby boomers live in our own little world," the white-haired man said, reading over my shoulder. He'd slipped his book into his pocket, but I could see the title: *Byzantium*.

"I'm about to squander my children's inheritance on a trip to Istanbul," I said, looking up to meet a pair of twinkling blue eyes in an interesting face, well-worn and full of character.

"Really?" The blue-eyed man smiled. I placed him as a retired teacher. His wife might be that Lucy Turnbull look-alike leafing through the brochures.

Or maybe the smart blonde in her thirties. Older men did attract younger women.

"Have you heard of Stannard Travel?" he went on. "Specialist in historical tours. There's one coming up with a focus on Byzantine architecture. Got a spare brochure somewhere…" He delved into his pockets, releasing a shower of coins, papers, keys and other debris.

The girls in the queue giggled, exchanging whispers. The man's face reddened as he stooped to gather up his belongings.

"I suppose we're typical boomers," I said, kneeling to help him. "We want the adventures we didn't have as kids. The far horizons. Really we should just sit quietly in a corner and get on with our knitting."

Mr. Blue Eyes gave a snort of laughter. I was glad I'd made him feel better.

I rescued a little plastic photo sleeve. A grey-haired woman gazed out with such love it made my heart flip over. How wonderful to have someone who felt like that about you.

"My wife, Sally," he said.

"She's lovely," I said.

"Number twenty-three!" called a Far Horizons staffer.

"That's me," he said. "Best of luck with your travels."

"You too." I watched him go to the desk, his back very straight. Maybe he was not a teacher, but a retired soldier. I flipped out my notebook and jotted a description for future reference. The lined face, the sensitive eyes the colour of…of gentians; the excellent posture. The fact that he had blushed. In the story, I would make him an ex-mountaineer, or an ex-fighter pilot…

I was still scribbling frantically when a voice cut into my thoughts.

"Number twenty-seven?"

I got up with a start, scattering my own belongings all over the floor. The ex-mountaineer or fighter pilot was nowhere in sight.

"Can I help?" The girls in jeans came over to pick up my notebook, pen, and glasses case. I thanked them. They'd probably been laughing earlier about their boyfriends, or work, or school. I had to stop reading articles about baby boomers. They were making me paranoid.

"Twenty-seven?"

Fifteen minutes later, with my credit card burning a hole in my wallet, I walked out of Far Horizons. The sales assistant hadn't been at all patronising. It had turned out she loved Turkish history too.

As for Stannard Travel, I'd asked for a brochure. Maybe I'd add their Byzantine Turkey tour to my itinerary. I'd probably get to see a lot more with a group. If the retired whatever-he-was and his wife were anything to go by, the company would be congenial. And if it would have been nice not to be travelling as a single, never mind that. My life was complicated enough these days without some man to be fitted in.

Outside Far Horizons, I almost tripped over a huge grey dog that was sitting obediently under the minaret poster. On a small table beyond this apparition stood a steaming cup of espresso. The rich aroma reminded me that I'd missed my post-lunch caffeine. There was a coffee shop right next to Far Horizons—how had I managed to miss that before?

"Please join us." It was him, Mr. Blue Eyes, seated on the other side of the alfresco table, the dog leash looped around his chair. "But maybe you don't like dogs. Timur, say hello nicely to the lady."

"Timur?" I queried, reaching to scratch the hound behind his oversized ears. "After the Mongolian warlord? I guess I was right about you the first time, when I placed you as a history teacher." A moment later, I felt a flush rise to my cheeks. I was talking as if he was an old friend, and I didn't even know the man's name. "Good boy, Timur," I muttered to cover my embarrassment.

"Do sit down." Blue Eyes didn't sound put out, just curious. "The coffee here's quite good. May I order one for you?"

"Thank you." It had been longer than I could remember since a man had offered to buy me coffee. It was a good feeling. "Espresso, please."

I sat down. Timur rested his long shaggy snout on my knee as if I were his long-lost buddy.

"So," said my human companion, "what was the second time?"

"What second time?"

"When I wasn't a history teacher." He signalled to a hip wait-person in black.

"Oh, dear. Now I'm going to embarrass myself. You were either a retired fighter pilot or a mountaineer. It's the posture, mostly. You've the look of an outdoor man."

"A fighter pilot? After you saw me drop my personal belongings all over the floor?"

"I did say retired." I smiled at him and received a charming grin in return.

"Sorry to disappoint you. I'm afraid I'm an accountant. Semi-retired; I do a little consulting work here and there. My name's Bill Stephenson, by the way." He reached out a hand to shake mine; his grip was strong and warm. "I did much better at guessing your occupation," he went on.

My brows rose sceptically.

"Romance novelist," Bill Stephenson said, deadpan. Then, before I could summon a reply, he added, "My wife adored your books, Ms. Summer. I know them cover to cover.'

"You read romance?" I asked in disbelief.

A kind of shadow came over Bill's face. "Sally died last year," he said. "Breast cancer; it was a pretty slow process. I did all sorts of things to distract her from the pain. She liked me to read aloud. We only just made it to the end of *Whisper*."

The arrival of my coffee allowed me a breathing space.

"I'm so sorry," I managed as the wait-person departed. "How sad."

"It's taken a long time to start coming to terms with it. A lot of soul-searching. Reading's helped. I have to admit that, on my own, I do favour history over romance. Of course, a novel that combined the two effectively would be irresistible, don't you think, Ms. Summer?"

"Funny you should say that." There had been an idea bubbling away in my mind ever since I'd seen the minaret poster: a sweeping romantic epic set in Byzantine Turkey. "By the way, Felicity Summer is a pseudonym. My real name's the far more prosaic Althea Brown. Call me Althea, please."

"It's an enchanting name, eh, Timur?" The dog grinned agreement, drooling on my best wool skirt. "As for the outdoor man, my main form of exercise is walking Timur. I keep planning to do more. When you're on your own, it's easy to put it off."

We talked about swimming and bushwalking. Over second coffees we exchanged family information and dissected the latest Tim Winton. The light was fading; the wait-person began wiping down tables. Bill was scribbling something on one of his many scraps of paper when my mobile rang. It was Bella, talking so loudly my companion could surely hear every word.

"Where *are* you, Mum? I thought you were going straight home after the hair salon, but I got the answering machine. I need you to come round and help with—"

"I'm having coffee with my accountant," I said primly.

"Who's that laughing in the background?" Bella asked suspiciously. "Mum? Where are you, really?"

A man passed with a terrier at his heels. Timur erupted into a frenzy of barking.

"Mum!" shrieked Bella. "Sean wasn't serious about the wolfhound! When we said do something for yourself, we didn't mean do something silly and irresponsible."

"I'm on a sort of date," I said calmly. "With a retired fighter pilot and a ferocious hunting dog." Bill was laughing too hard to write. The wait-person stared at us as if we were crazy.

Stunned silence from the mobile. Then Bella said, "You're joking."

"Not at all," I said as Bill finished writing his phone number and slid the paper across to me. "Didn't you know baby boomers have no sense of humour? It's all right, Bella. Trust your mother. I'll be over later to help you with whatever it is. Then I'm starting a fitness campaign. Lots of walks. And then I'm going to Turkey." I glanced over into Bill's mischievous blue eyes, his comfortably lived-in face, his kind smile. "And then …"

Under another name, Olivette Devaux is an award-winning Amazon bestseller. This pen name is dedicated to romantic fiction, both LGBT and "straight." Formerly a political refugee from Czechoslovakia, she writes thrillers, recent-historical stories, and strange fiction informed by her world travels. She now lives with her family in Pittsburgh, where she forages wild mushrooms, paints, and creates new worlds. This story is a stand-alone read from her Disorderly Elements world. Its characters are based on old Central European legendary creatures. This story takes place between Book 1, Like a Rock *and Book 2,* Like a Torrent"

THE FORBIDDEN KISS OF LIFE

(A Disorderly Elements Short Story)

by Olivette Devaux

The air was fresh with the tongues of autumn fog which lapped at the surface of the Vltava River like playful dogs. The sun had not quite come up yet, but the darkness of the post-equinox night broke with a swath of a pale gray stripe of light to the east. The sky brightened grudgingly, heavy with the rain to come.

This Saturday morning, the streets of Prague were still. The locals were sleeping in, securely warm behind closed doors. Their coffee would await them, and pastries, but that would come later. For now, Ash watched Teresa, his cousin as well as a young rusalka-in-training.

Back in the States, Ash was an elementalist. A water-whisperer. Rivers and streams spoke to him, and sometimes, they obeyed his polite requests. Here in Bohemia, however, he was called a *vodník*, a waterman. The term harkened back to old fairy tales, and even nowadays, children were warned to stay away from swift-moving streams.

"Don't go in, the *vodník* would drown you." The cautionary words were as commonplace as saying "Gesundheit" when someone sneezed.

He was appalled. He would never drown anyone. Of course, he'd never capture their soul and keep it under an upside-down teacup. No, he would not make a collection to show off, nor would he use the souls of others to bolster his own power. When their elderly aunt told stories of the days when their kind ruled the rivers, he learned that even though Teresa was just another water elementalist in the States, here she was a *rusalka*, a being that might lure a swimmer into the deep. The opera Rusalka formed a part of the nation's consciousness.

Ash looked to the other bank of the river, where the old buildings of Kampa island rose from the fog. He was an elementalist, not a *vodník*.

The whole soul-stealing idea was preposterous. It was a concept as antiquated as coal-powered stoves, and those days were long gone. The soot of the twentieth century had been washed off by a new era, one full of computers, cell phones and organic apples from nearby orchards. These changes had pushed out the old ways, which is why Ash Ravenna, a U.S. citizen, was teaching his young cousins in the old country to develop their innate gifts. He didn't speak much Czech, but most of the young'uns took English in school and acted as his enthusiastic interpreters.

In turn, he tried to unravel their familial relationships, learning that Teresa was his second cousin once removed and that the Italian side of his family might have been responsible for his surname, but had contributed absolutely nothing to his water-sense.

One of the most important things he taught was discretion. Under the now-defunct communist regime, their talents had been waved off as mere superstitions. Claiming to be a water-whisperer, or a fairy-tale water spirit, would have landed people in a psychiatric ward. Or, even worse, it would've made them a subject of secret experiments. Nobody wanted to be captured, imprisoned, and weaponized.

The "special powers" of their kind were a closely guarded secret.

These thoughts ran through Ash's mind even as he hovered five feet under the water's dim surface. Here he would banish old fears and feel the gentle caress of the river's current. She would wash off his stress, his fretful concern. Here he would smell only the decaying vegetation spiced with a hint of methane from the deep layers of river mud, and he would ignore the alarming levels of PCBs and heavy metals—a vestige of a less enlightened era—which tingled his transformed skin with pinpricks of information.

The rivers were getting cleaner, but just like back in the States, their condition was far from perfect. The heavy, silt-laden flow of the Vltava River snaked her way through Prague, her brown-green body cascading down the locks and weirs, the waves on her surface reflecting the earliest glimmer of this morning's autumnal light.

Ash Ravenna glanced at his young apprentice through the water. She got faster at changing her skin structure, fast enough so that the air in her lungs wouldn't run out before she could absorb the needed oxygen directly from the stream. This was a big step for her because Teresa came to river-walking late. Had she only been carried under the waves as a baby in her mother's arms, just like Ash had been…but despite missing her early window of opportunity to learn naturally, Teresa was determined, and he was hell-bent to teach her all he could despite their awkward Czech-English interface on land.

The language barrier didn't matter here, under the surface. Here, their minds touched and thoughts flowed back and forth in a fluid rapport, allowing their kind to stay under and still communicate for hours at a time.

This was a helpful skill to have, because Teresa could last in the watery realm for up to thirty-five minutes now, a formidable accomplishment considering that an experienced, normal human with a fairly large lung capacity did well if they stayed under for more than two minutes.

He watched her slide along the contours of the riverbed, floating, navigating the current above the muddy river bottom, eyeing the half-buried human artifacts with great curiosity. He watched her stroke the rough ridges of a truck tire with a frown on her face. Clouds of silt billowed into the stream, obscuring his vision.

Sorry. Her thought-voice was without an accent, unlike her English on dry land.

That's okay, he thought back. *You'll get used to this. The silt is deep, especially when the rivers are bound by dams. See how the impoundment area stretches upstream?*

He did not need to explain what an impoundment was, because when they exchanged their thoughts, visual impressions often followed. From the way she looked upstream, Ash knew that Teresa was imagining—and feeling—all the backed-up water which was now being contained by a weir fifty meters north of them, right in the middle of Prague and near the ancient Charles Bridge. Except here, under the stoic eyes of the stone saints that had stood on the bridge for centuries, the impoundment only meant a high water precariously contained by the riverbanks, which were built up into stone walls that held streets and boulevards. Though busy with pedestrians and zooming cars during the day, the city was still asleep.

Ash turned his attention back to the river and her flow. Once the river became bound by the engineering props of human activity and harnessed to work tirelessly without spilling from her banks, she began to sicken.

Pollution issues were easier to address and easier to resolve than having people agree to the removal of the dams, the locks, and the weirs that had been a part of their environment ever since they could remember, and which they believed would prevent flooding—but of course, that was a poorly understood myth. At best, these antiquated structures caused the river to silt up, and at worst they worsened the flooding they were thought to prevent.

He saw Teresa strike out toward an island to their left with a swift kick, and Ash knew that it was time for her to revert.

He caught up with ease and swam behind her, heedless of the turbulence that stirred up the endless supply of mud in his passing. Nobody would see them six feet under the surface. And if they were careful, nobody would see two naked people climb out of the river and disappear into the bushes, the concealing foliage of which had turned yellow and red with nighttime frost.

Now that they were on dry land, Teresa watched her skin shift from that pearly and almost opalescent sheen of a gas-permeable membrane into a more protective dry-land skin familiar to regular people. She gasped, forcing her lungs to draw the crisp autumn air now that her skin stopped absorbing the oxygen her body craved.

She glanced around, looking for her towel. The nip in the air did not bother her in her water form, but as soon as her skin texture normalized, goosebumps sprang up and she began to shiver.

"Here you go," Ash said as he handed her a blanket. "It makes no sense to dry and get dressed since we are going back in again."

She made a face. "I wish I could stay under as long as you," she said. "I thought we would swim upriver!"

"And we will," Ash said with a bemused smile, "but you were interested in treasure hunting, which is perfectly fine." He pulled a thermos bottle out of his backpack, opened it, and poured an amber colored steaming liquid into the lid that doubled as a drinking cup. "Here, have some tea." He pushed the cup in her direction, she gratefully accepted it. Warm, not nearly as hot as the steam would indicate, and most especially, sweet. Once her core warmed up enough so she could think again and her shivers subsided, Teresa handed the cup back to him. His presence and his advice had been invaluable. The river-walking they were doing now was the culmination of two months of dry land training, during which Teresa had to control her mind and her body both.

Breathe. Ground and center.

"Ground and center," Ash said to remind her of the basics, echoing her thoughts.

She nodded, arranged her body in half-lotus position while still cocooned in Ash's blue and white blanket, and settled her mind. Within moments, as air left her body in smooth and tranquil exhales, she felt the cold leave her as though someone lifted a wet towel off her shoulders. Only a few minutes later, Teresa opened her eyes and smiled. "I'm ready to go in again if you are!"

Jarda jogged up the bridge and looked around. The fog was threatening to disperse, and he didn't want his swan-song dive to be visible. Nobody would bear him witness today, because this early on a foggy Saturday morning, not even the dog walkers were out yet.

He crested the highest part of the bridge, leaned against the stone and iron railing that harkened back to the aesthetic of the ancient Austro-Hungarian Empire, and looked downstream. The ancient Charles Bridge marked a dark silhouette in the fog, as though its mass formed an insurmountable barrier downstream. He had decided not to jump off the Charles Bridge, because on a morning like this he was likely to run into a photographer or two who were out there, hunting for a shot without the ubiquitous crowds of tourists that clogged it during the day.

This particular bridge was further upstream and had no such issues. There were no statues, no tourists. Only the Dancing Building swirled in its asymmetrical swoops of concrete and panes of glass to his left. Joyful and modern, some denizens of Prague thought it was a fun statement, while others considered it an eyesore that did not quite fit next to the traditional neo-classical architecture.

He was like the Dancing Building—a source of controversy for everyone who knew him. He didn't fit, and he was trouble, and he was danger in his crazed and deluded mind.

Just as some old-timers had hoped that the modernistic heap of concrete and glass would fall into the river, Jarda knew his family's life would be better without him.

Just leaving didn't cut it, though. No matter where he would go, he would still see things that weren't there, scary freaky illusions of conflagrations, of burning buildings, of heat accumulating deep underground.

He would still wake up in a bed with scorched sheets and the reek of singed cotton sheets and melted polyester batting of the mattress when he had one of his fire dreams. The day would come when he would set the whole building ablaze and kill every living thing in it.

He'd rather kill himself.

He had left his phone and wallet home along with his leather jewelry, and he had already chucked his train boarding pass.

He left his good leather jacket behind—his brother had always coveted it.

His disappearance would be a mystery. Nobody would connect a nameless drowned man in Prague to a troubled young electrician who disappeared from Pilsen. The fire dreams would no longer haunt his nights and there would be no need to fear he would kill his family, or a whole apartment building full of more than two hundred sleeping souls. They wouldn't fall victim to the curse he had been, to date, able to disguise as a string of "smoking in bed" accidents.

Jarda zipped up his hoodie and kicked the railing with his steel-toe construction boot. The more clothes he wore, the easier he'd go down. He took one last look up and down the banks of the river, soaked in the view of the bridges that spanned her and the hills that began to peek from within the fog.

The sun lit up the sky to the east.

It was time.

He scrambled up the scroll-work of the metal railing and stood up on the granite pillar that anchored it.

Good-bye, fire dreams.

He pushed off. Adrenaline spiked through his veins as the cold air hit his face, and with that adrenaline came fire.

The shoulders of his hoodie burst into flames.

He had just a split-second to enjoy the satisfaction of knowing that this was the last fire he would ever set, then his boots hit the surface.

A splash, then cold water rushing into his jeans, a hiss as the hated fire died out.

The silence, punctuated by the unexpected noise of his own air bubbles, was more startling than the fall.

He let some of his air escape, sacrificing a measure of oxygen—he had predicted the panic he was feeling now and fought the urge to kick and swim himself back to the surface.

He hit the bottom and kept going, sinking into the mud and muck that had been accumulating at the bottom of the river, waiting for him as though by design.

He smiled. Buried to his ribs, there was no getting out of here no matter how hard his survival instinct would kick in. One glance up, one last glance at the sun that broke through the fog up above. The green and gold of the water column was topped by the sky itself. A reflection, he realized. A reflection of the clouds above, first pale gray, then burning with a brilliance he would never see again.

He had made his peace with that weeks ago. He was stuck in the river mud at least five meters under the surface, watching the play of the day's first sunlight upon the waves.

It was so lovely, so playful and healing. He didn't have the heart—or the courage—to inhale water on purpose. Instead, he quietly enjoyed the last glorious display of the fire that was now forbidden

him and waited for the river to force him to take a breath again.

Ash and Teresa were upstream of the island and of the statue that decorated its tip and close to the other bridge. Ash had no trouble orienting himself in the river, whose current told him what passed above and what contours lay below. This old river whispered of battles fought long time ago, of kings on horses. She showed glimpses of men who floated rafts of lumber through Prague before the river had been shackled by dams and weirs.

She whispered to him of life, and of death, and Ash had trouble telling the old histories apart from the more recent news.

He tore away from the torrent of information and focused on the present. Teresa swam ahead of him, pushing out of her own comfort zone. His presence made that possible, and his attention on her energies made it safe.

Still doing okay? He thought in her direction.

Yes. A pause, then, *Oh, shit!*

He felt the presence of another before he saw him, but Teresa was closer, close enough to feel the river part as the jumper sliced through the water and got stuck in sediment below.

Ash had come upon jumpers like that before, but he had never been there when it happened. He had always wondered what made them do it, and he felt a stab of regret as their bodies ripened and decomposed. He always let them be, knowing that the gases of decomposition would pluck the jumper out of the mud and float the body to the surface, where the authorities would take over.

Except this one was still alive.

Teresa kicked out, shooting forward like a fish and, suddenly, her intent was all too clear.

No! Don't! Ash followed her with all his might. *We aren't allowed to interfere.*

But he'll die, she responded in a voice that was all too calm. Stubbornly calm.

Ash didn't want him to die, but he didn't want them to be discovered either. He sent a vision of a body being burned at stake.

She didn't even bother turning his way. *He's not like that,* she sent. Ash watched her shoot up to the surface, take a lungful of fresh air, then fight her way down with her more buoyant weight. She grabbed the man's head, and as he exhaled the last of his spent air and was about to take in water, she kissed him.

This was the forbidden kiss of life; the one Ash had always been taught to avoid. It wasn't that the water-whisperers drowned people—they didn't—but they didn't want to be discovered by those they rescue, who would later fear them.

The man got his air. His eyes fluttered open as he watched Teresa with tranquil acceptance.

She tried to pull on his shoulders now. A futile effort. The river mud had a good bit of suction to it, and it would take more than just a few tugs to extricate anything or anyone.

Ash, come on, help me save him!

Old schooling battled with the knowledge that these were different times. Secrecy was still of paramount importance, but they had been in the water for quite a while, and he knew that Tessa's skin would soon want to transform.

The sun was out.

The fog would burn off, and people would soon spill into the streets.

Saving this poor, misguided man would be faster if he helped. They'd be out of the water and dressed, looking normal, if he helped. And, yes, he would feel less regret if he helped.

Keep giving him air and watch what I do, he said, *and* felt her assent as he looked upstream. Slowly, and not without fear, Ash lowered the shields that protected the core of his being from other energies.

And then he felt it. The suicide man glowed with a power-signature of his own. He was one of them, and if the chaos of his mind was any indication, he was entirely untrained.

Poor guy thinks he's going mad, Ash thought as he settled into a trance.

The river was heavy in his mind, heavy and old, and powerful.

More current here, he requested, aiming the sole focus of his mind at the mud that had trapped the jumper's chest, his hips.

The visions of old battles receded, and now he saw a pale green light in its place. Had the river been a person, he would have called it her aura. The light brightened above the mud, and the particles began to move faster as the speed of the current increased.

If Teresa could keep bringing fresh air, and if he could maintain his focus, then maybe—just maybe—they would deny this man his watery grave.

He would never be a *vodník*—he would never suck the soul out of a drowning man. Secrecy be damned, Ash resolved. He'd do anything he could to help.

Anger gave her strength as she brought yet another lungful of air to the man down below. Still seething at Ash for his initial reticence, she fueled her resolve with the adrenaline of her righteous rage. It wasn't as though a crowd of peasants would chase them around with pitchforks. This wasn't the middle ages, after all.

She let the jumper exhale his loud, spent bubbles and gave him another kiss of life, just about forcing extra oxygen into his lungs.

He was aware of her. His eyes followed her with an incredulous expression, and for a split-second she had felt what Ash called a "power-signature."

Regular people weren't supposed to have one, but after the way Ash had hesitated to save this man, Teresa's esteem of his opinion had taken a bit of a dive. Maybe Ash didn't know everything. Maybe regular humans had a power signature, except not everyone could see it. She spent only a stray thought on this as she kicked her way back to the surface. If he survived, she would sit and meditate, and *feel* this man. See what he was made of. Was he attuned to one element, or several? Was *he* aware of *her* power signature?

The current grew in strength and speed so fast, she had trouble making it to her jumper. He needed more air, but her legs grew weary, and her arms faltered with fatigue.

What if she…? Yes! She was a rusalka, after all. She had been shown how to do that one forbidden thing. The old thing, which had left Ash so appalled when he had heard ancient whispers of it all those weeks ago.

Teresa fought her way to the jumper.

She grabbed his head, pressed their lips together, and inhaled.

A hot, seething ember of life spilled into her mouth. So much power, so much strength. Such fire in it, and if she let it settle in her body, she would possess all that power, all that fire.

Water and fire. The possibilities were dizzying.

The temptation was strong, and the power on her tongue was like a gulp of water to a woman dying in the desert.

Teresa! No! Ash's anguished voice echoed in her mind, grounding her. Reminding her who she was, and what she had resolved to do.

She nodded. *Don't worry,* she thought back at him. *I'm not consuming him. This will work fine.*

Let's pull him out! Ash was in her mind again, somehow louder and clearer than ever before.

She grabbed the man's sleeves, keeping her mouth shut and his soul safely within herself, and pulled.

Ash was next to her, his slick arm sliding against her shoulder. His inner light blazed like a high-powered lamp, all blue and green and so bright it hurt. The river was strong now, and fierce, and it ripped at her hair and threatened to separate her from the man she meant to rescue.

One more push—a blaze of light—and they were loose, tumbling upside down in a torrent of muddy water.

She never let go.

The island's to the right, Ash nudged her, and as she righted herself, she kicked out again and pulled with all her strength. Never in her short life did she want anything more than to see this man survive.

Death was so beautiful, Jarda realized as she floated toward him. Death was not a grim reaper, a bare and grinning skull under his black cloak. It was a girl, naked skin shimmering in the water, long hair flowing past her waist. Like a rusalka—a water spirit from children's fairy tales.

Death didn't behead with an old, rusty scythe. No, Death kissed and gave air, smoothing the transfer between the Land of the Living, and the other place. She was Death, kissed by the sunbeam that lit up the water column with new hope. She was Death, and she glowed with that same light, all green like the glow of the river, and gold like the sun, and silver like a pale moon in the sky. Death was magic, and Jarda didn't regret his choice for a single moment. There were surely worse ways to go than being kissed by Death's soft lips, feeling Death's secure grip on his shoulder as she grabbed him and pulled.

Wait, she had help. A minion, an underling of some kind. And he, too, glowed, but not like the sun and the moon. No, he was dark and beautiful, and fearsome.

And strong.

His last thoughts were of his family. He had hoped his body would never be identified. He had hoped his family would all think he's fine, adventuring in foreign lands and coming back someday. He had hoped they would forgive him for never writing.

They wouldn't have understood.

The algae slicked the stones by this end of the island, and exhausted and hurting from their exertion, Ash tried hard not to scratch his transformed skin on them before it dried. Then he realized Teresa might have the same urge.

Between huffs and puff of effort, he broke their silence. "Don't ever…scratch…your water-skin. On rocks and…stuff."

Why? Still in her water-skin, she thought instead of speaking.

"Heals worse than if you scratch it on dry land."

Ash was acutely aware of their nudity now that the sun had burned the fog off the river, and that sound of cars and faraway tramways filled the air. "Let's drag him out of sight," he said.

Lips still pressed together, she nodded. Moments later, they were surrounded by bushes and trees. A pair of swans, barely visible through the foliage, fought the burst of swift current to stay near their nest. Ash dropped to his knees and drew a deep breath, steadying himself on an exhale. "Let's see if he has a pulse."

Teresa pushed him aside, bent over the man, and latched her lips over his own.

He was dead—he had been dead—but as she relinquished his soul and let it resettle in his inert body, the indigo receded from his lips, replaced by a faint pink.

She propped up his shoulder and turned him to the side. He coughed. A bit of water spilled out, and then he drew a wheezing, panicked breath.

She let him settle on his back again. Ash saw her gasp with fatigue.

"You should have told me what you wanted me to do," he said. "You don't have to do everything on your own."

Their eyes met. Hers had a haunted, terrified look, as though she had seen and felt that which cannot be unseen. "I couldn't open my mouth," she whispered, leaning close to Ash's ear. "I didn't want his soul to get out."

"Really?" Ash shuddered. "But…but that was just a legend. A fairy tale."

A wan smile crossed her face. "What are we, but a fairy tale?"

Ash saw their charge was young, in his early twenties at the most. His clothing, all soaked and charred, was what made him so hard to get out of the water.

"He's breathing," Teresa said. "And we'll need our things." She gave Ash an expectant look.

"I'll go get it," he said and jogged to the downstream side of the island. They had been lucky this far, but Ash didn't want to risk fielding questions as to why they were swimming in the river that cut through the capital, in October, and naked.

The path was soft with leaves under his feet, and Ash was now grateful for the smells of the city because even diesel exhaust grounded him in reality. The scent of fresh bread reminded him of his physical needs. He was just a guy now, a regular man struggling into his clothes because he hadn't dried off properly. He tied his sneakers, grabbed the blanket and towels and Teresa's tidy pile of clothing, and ran back.

The man was awake now, shivering and babbling. Even though Ash was picking up new Czech words and phrases every day, his speech was too fast to understand. He set her clothes down and tossed Teresa a towel along with a questioning look.

"He thinks I'm Death and this is…what is the word?"

"Heaven? Hell?" Ash suggested.

"Kind of. A place after death." She toweled herself off without any shyness.

Soon she was dressed in her blue tracksuit, yoga slippers on her feet and her hair bound in a purple towel turban. "We need to dry him," she said, searching for English words.

"Yes. We will strip him and dry him, and find him dry clothes," Ash said. "If you want, I'll do it and you can go get some of my things. They will be big on him, but they will do the job."

"I don't want to leave him."

"I don't want to leave you alone with him." Ash's protective instincts reared. "We don't know what he

is capable of…but we know what he is. A Fire Man. I suspect he's untrained and that makes him potentially dangerous."

"I'm strong, don't worry. And he thinks I'm Death!" Her stubborn expression was a well-known staple, but that soft look in her eyes was as new as it was unexpected.

Now that he was naked and wrapped in a blue and white blanket, Jarda was less cold than when he had been wearing his clammy clothes. Death was sitting on a throne made of a fallen tree, and the gold light he had seen before had diminished to just a glimmer, as though the sun was playing tricks on his mind as it filtered through the yellow leaves.

Fancy that, having fall-colored leaves in the afterlife. Or wherever he was.

Death now wore an imposing turban on her head, which made him wonder whether the head-dress had any religious significance.

"What's your name?" she asked.

That surprised him. Didn't she know whose life she had taken? "Jarda," he said, and squinted his eyes against the golden glow. "Where am I?"

She hesitated. "Where do you think you are?"

"Maybe some kind of an afterlife, but…wait." He turned his head toward the nearby shore, where the traffic had thickened. "That sounded like a car horn. There should be no traffic in the afterlife!"

"Maybe you're in hell," she suggested seriously. "Maybe there's traffic all the time!"

"Well, I'm cold and hungry, so maybe this is hell after all." He thought back. "But I remember you from the river. From underwater. And you were swimming, with long hair…" He gave her a once-over, afraid to ogle, but still unable to forget her nude body and the way she cut through the water like a fish.

A stone dug through the blanket, right into his butt. The discomfort it caused was reassuring. He caught a whiff of diesel, and maybe a scent of fresh-baked bread. "Wow. I think I'm alive."

She smiled.

"But if I'm alive, then you're not Death. You're real. I mean, you're a real person." He recalled his mission. He was supposed to be dead now, deep underwater and not a danger to others anymore. Except he wasn't, and that made him angry. "You shouldn't have rescued me," he said.

To his surprise, she didn't say anything. She settled in a lotus position, looking like a model on a yoga class poster, and closed her eyes halfway. She breathed, and as she did, Jarda felt a curious feeling of *other* in his mind.

"What are you doing?" he whispered.

She remained silent, focused on him. It occurred to him that he should just get up and leave. He could go home all wet, maybe hitchhike, and jump into the river again some other time. Maybe he should've picked a different place—but there was no way he could have known these crazy skinny-dippers would even be here.

He sat, enjoying the glow around her, even though it was just the sun filtering through yellow leaves. He sat, enjoying her single-minded focus on him, her lovely face, her serious expression, as though she was doing something important.

Most of all, he liked to think back to his time underwater, when the river had been alight with green energy and she was all bright and sunny and powerful, kissing him into what he had believed was the Other Side.

Time passed, and her dark minion returned with a canvas shopping bag. "I brought you some clothes," he said quietly as he set it down by Jarda's feet. Then he looked at the girl who was not Death and sighed. "Okay, tell me what you're seeing."

Teresa knew this was no ordinary man. She had not suffered through countless meditation sessions in vain, and Jarda, who still thought she was Death, and beautiful, made a slew of butterflies panic in her stomach. He was no ordinary man because he made her heart race, and because when she had held his soul in hers, she had become privy to his deepest fears.

"Well?" Ash prodded.

"He is one of us," she said with certainty. "He has no shields at all. He doesn't know how to ground and center, and he is not water or wind, like the others. I don't know what he is." She did not feel entitled to voice Jarda's secrets, his memory of a burning bed, or his terrifying fear of hurting those he loved.

Ash knelt on the wet leaves and gave the man a long look. "He is fire."

She almost jumped—so much for her protective urge—but Jarda didn't react, which told her that a language barrier might be an issue. Not everyone took to learning English, after all. She translated. "You are fire, he says."

He jerked his head up. "What? But... that's all in my head."

Teresa sighed. This was going to be an exhausting conversation, with her doing all the translating. "I am hungry. How about we go get some coffee and some pastries, and we can talk?"

Jarda gave her a panicked look. Of course, a suicide wouldn't have any money on him.

"My treat," she said generously. "And don't worry, Ash bought you clothes that would fit."

Two weeks later, Ash sat at the table with the adults in the family, while Teresa was leading a meditation session for her younger cousins. Jarda was the oldest of the group and the least experienced, but he hung on her every word.

He resonated with her, and Ash could feel it.

"I still think it's not natural, a rusalka taking up with a fire-man," her aunt whispered over her coffee. "We should stick to our own."

For the first time ever, Ash revealed what this side of his extended family did not yet know. "I'm water, but my partner? He is earth and fire."

The words fell onto a silent, fertile ground. His uncles, aunts, and distant cousins eyed him curiously, keeping their counsel and thinking so hard Ash could almost hear the gears turning.

"She is turning into a good teacher," he said, propping Teresa up as much as he could prior to his departure. "And Jarda's accidents are at a minimum. Soon he won't have to sleep in the tent anymore."

"He helped the guys wire the shop in the basement." The aunt's approval was like one of a mother whose daughter had found a man who knew how to do things.

Ash nodded. "That's good." They didn't need to know that Teresa and Jarda were inseparable. They also didn't need to know that their love wasn't one at first sight, as much as at first breath. Because when a rusalka breathes in a fire-man's soul for safekeeping, she gets to weigh that soul upon her tongue. Examine it. And in this case, she found it...more than palatable.

And when a fire-man is forced to reside within a water-whisperer's soul, surrounded by an alien and hostile element only to come out of it alive, he will live with his heart full of trust

Only from trust can true love spring—and he knew that from personal experience.

Suddenly homesick, Ash thought of his own true love.

Three more days. He could hardly wait.

The Disorderly Elements series:

- LIKE A ROCK (Book 1)
- ZERO POWER SIGNATURE (Short story from Cooper's childhood)
- LIKE A TORRENT (Book 2)
  WITHIN A CROWDED BLADE (Short story about what really happened to Jared in Book 2)
- LIKE A SURGE (Book 3)
- LIKE A PHOENIX (Book 4)
- THREE SOLSTICE GIFTS (Short holiday story, takes place during Phoenix)

D. H. Hendrickson has published two hockey romance novels, Body Check *and* No Defense, *as well as four other novels (writing as David H. Hendrickson). His novel* Offside *has been adopted for high school student required reading. His short fiction has appeared in* Ellery Queen's Mystery Magazine, Pulphouse, *and numerous anthologies, including multiple issues of* Fiction River. *His story "Death in the Serengeti" has been selected for* Best American Mystery Stories 2018. *Hendrickson has published over fifteen hundred works of nonfiction, most recently* Travis Roy: Quadriplegia and a Life of Purpose. *He has been honored with the Joe Concannon Hockey East Media Award and the Murray Kramer Scarlet Quill Award. Follow him at www.hendricksonwriter.com.*

FROM A DRY, BITTER STREAM COMES THE SWEETEST OF FOUNTAINS

by D. H. Hendrickson

And so, it was that in the land of the Israelites, there was a maiden by the name of Deborah and she was of fair countenance and a stature almost unto a man. For as far as her name was known, men of good will held her in highest regard for she honored her father, Zilpar, and all her kin. She tended Zilpar's sheep which numbered thirty and seven, for Zilpar had not been blessed with a son.

Thus, had the Lord God of Israel cursed him, Zilpar cried out at the end of each day, tearing at his raiment and gnashing his teeth for two of his wives were barren and the other two had given him none but three daughters, of which Deborah was the eldest.

"Why must thou persecute me?" he cried each night from outside the family's tents, ten strides from where the two younger girls huddled against Deborah in their own tent, her arms protectively wrapped about them. With the dirt and clay of the ground smeared upon his face and into the strands of his thick beard, he would say to the heavens, "You have denied me a son to whom I can extend my inheritance and burdened me instead with three daughters, only Deborah of whom is beautiful and even she will cost me many oxen to rid of in marriage."

Deborah did hold these words in her heart, for they had been spoken so many times before. She counselled her sisters, Eulanna, aged twelve and with darkened hair, and Sophilia, aged nine with hair of fiery red. They whispered words to Deborah of their injured pride, "Are we less than the beasts of the field. Are we like the dung they leave in their wake?"

Deborah wiped away their tears and comforted their sorrows, patting their heads, covered by veils of harsh, coarse fabric the color of sand, like her own, atop loose robes of the same color, held tight at the waist.

"You know not whereof you speak, for you are young and do not know the law," Deborah said. "No child, especially a daughter, may challenge Father. It is the law."

But Deborah harbored the same thoughts as her sisters, differing only in her wisdom to speak not the words.

❖

After a long journey into a far-off land, Lashem returned to the land of his people, the Israelites, riding aboard a donkey loaded down with his belongings. The trip had been long and hard, and he grieved when he found that his kin had left for better lands. The hot summer sun had baked the earth dry and turned all the grass the color of yellow and brown and made it as brittle as long, dead twigs. In the last day, he had come upon beasts lying on their sides, their chests heaving and near unto death for lack of water, their coats matted with blood, flies buzzing about them even as their stench filled the air.

Knowing not where to go with his people departed, he continued to the east and when he came over a ridge that overlooked a dark brown grassy plain, he saw a maiden tending a flock of sheep, thirty or forty strong. She was fair to look upon, pleasing to the eye as she stood in her sand-colored robes and veil, using a staff that rose almost to the height of her full stature to prod the animals in the way they were to go. And though his very bones were tired, and his body ached for want of food and drink, he felt his heart lightened.

But the maiden saw him with alarm. Her eyes widened, and she cried out in fear. She turned and fled.

"This way! Follow me!" she yelled to the sheep, waving for them to join her.

Lashem called out, but she appeared not to hear.

Several of the sheep did not follow her, and when she looked and saw that it was true, she was sorely vexed. To the sheep that were with her, she pointed the way to go, then ran back for those that had not followed.

"Move!" she yelled at them and swung her staff to force them in the way to go. The last of them trotted in the right direction and the maiden quickened her stride.

"Be not afraid!" Lashem called out again, still riding upon the slow-moving donkey. "I mean you no harm."

The maiden stopped, and again Lashem was struck by her beauty. His heart beat faster, even as she stood to face him and held out her staff with both hands before her as if to ward him off.

"Come no closer," she said. "My father is nearby, just over the next ridge. He will fight you to the death to protect my honor."

"Your honor is in no danger, my fair maiden," Lashem said, stopping the donkey. He slid aside the rough cloth that covered his face, protecting it from the harsh overhead sun. He scratched his sandy colored beard and smiled. "I, too, am an Israelite. My name is Lashem, son of Nahol. I have returned from a long journey only to find my people, the people of Harrar, departed. No trace of them remains. And so I am alone. But you and I serve the same God, the Lord God Jehovah. Fear me not."

The maiden didn't move. Lashem's donkey swayed but moved no closer. Finally, she spoke, though in a halting, uncertain voice.

"Over the next ridge behind me, there is a well," she said. "But a huge stone covers it, one too heavy for me to move. Follow me but come no closer than your distance of one hundred paces and fifty. I will take my flock to the other side of it. If you can move aside the stone, you may drink of the water and draw, too, enough for me and my flock and we will be grateful. I will show you to my father's house and we will give you food to eat and a place to sleep."

And though the stone was great and Lashem could not move it without the help of his donkey, he and the beast pulled the stone aside and they all did drink, man, woman, donkey, and sheep alike, drawing up bucket after bucket until they all were filled. The water was cold and pure, and tasted as sweet as honey as it washed away the dry grit in Lashem's mouth. The maiden, whose name was Deborah, thanked him in the name of her father, even while keeping her distance to one hundred paces and fifty.

"I thought your father was just over the last ridge," Lashem said, a smile curling again on his lips.

The maiden, Deborah, looked confused. She cocked her head at him as all about her the sheep bleated. "I do not understand."

"You said before that your father was here on this ridge, and that he would slay me if I disgraced your honor," Lashem said, grinning even more broadly now. He spread his arms now. "I see him not. I believe the fair maiden didst tell me a lie."

Lashem watched with amusement as the skin left exposed by the maiden's veil colored a deep red.

"I knew not whether I might trust you," she said.

"Now you know, I hope, that my word is true," he said. "Just as I now know your own is not."

❖

Deborah felt her face grow hot at the stranger's jest. And yet his own body shook with such merriment that she could not help but join him in laughter as well. She enjoyed being with this man, though she reminded herself to maintain the distance demanded by custom to uphold a maiden's honor. Even so, the collar of her robes grew tight about her neck. The heat of her own breath grew hot beneath her veil.

Fearing that her immodesty had grown too great, Deborah took her staff and prodded the sheep. "Come, follow me," she said to Lashem. "The sun is still high, and the sheep must still graze about the pasture, but we will go to my father's abode."

And so Lashem and his donkey moved the stone back atop the well so that it would not dry up and in time they returned to the tents where her father waited.

❖

Lashem had feared no man until the evil spirit came upon Zilpar. The man had greeted him with the affection of one Israelite to another, especially one from so close as Harrar, embracing him and kissing him upon the cheek.

They sat beneath a sycamore tree, its thick canopy shielding them from the setting sun, its fresh, clean scents a welcome change from the rank odor of the sheep and his own donkey. A light breeze wafted through the air.

"Deborah will bring us our bread and porridge," Zilpar said. "She will be but a while."

"She tends the flocks *and* cooks your meals?" Lashem asked.

"Yes," Zilpar said. "I have no sons to work the fields, no sons to tend the flocks. Deborah must do that work, for she is the oldest of my three daughters."

And yet she also cooked the meals? Lashem wondered at that. It seemed a burden heavier than he had seen before. He had met her just this very day, yet already he felt protective of her and disliked that she had been burdened so.

Careful not to betray the hospitality of his host, Lashem asked, "How many wives have you been blessed with?"

Anger flared in Zilpar's eyes. He drew air in noisily through his wide nostrils.

"I had four, but none remain," he said. "My first was my most beloved. She gave birth to Deborah, but two years later died during childbirth, attempting to give me my one and only son. But they both died, and I took another wife. She bore me but my other two daughters, then died of a fever. I took a third wife and a fourth, but they both proved barren and quarrelsome, so I sent them both back to their fathers."

Lashem nodded, then looked upon Deborah as she brought them bread to eat. She was even more lovely than he had thought when she stood amongst the flocks, leaning against her staff, already weary with so much of her day's work still to come.

"In truth, I was cursed with three of the four wives," Zilpar said, and spat on the ground. "Maybe all four. Even my most beloved wife could not give to me a living son. Not one son!" he thundered. "What good were they?"

Zilpar spread wide his hands and looked to the heavens as the evil spirit overtook him.

"You have cursed me since the day that I was born," he screamed to the clouds. "I was accursed with a father who beat me for no reason. I was accursed with weak eyesight so that as a boy I had to do the work of my sisters instead of a man's work. And then I was accursed with four wives who gave me nothing but three daughters. No one to grant my inheritance. They gave me nothing!"

Lashem attempted to interrupt with words of praise for Deborah but was cut off before he started.

"You have not just cursed me, but all of your people," Zilpar cried, shaking his fist to the skies. "Without water falling from the heavens, our fields turn brown and die, our crops fail. Dust fills our nostrils. Our sustenance is but watery broth."

Zilpar stood, his face choked with rage. "Lord God of Israel, I curse you!"

Lashem climbed to his feet in stunned silence as Deborah rushed to her father's side.

"Father, no! You know not of what you speak," she said. "Say not such an evil thing! You must be silent before the Lord God himself strikes you dead. We bore witness ourselves to His wrath. Did he not strike down Vekial with a bolt of fire from the heavens for his sins? Was not Vekial turned into a ball of flame, blackened into a burned-out husk? Would you seek God's vengeance so?"

"If it were so, at least the heavens would be opened and the fields turned to green," Zilpar cried. "At least all of our people would not go hungry, and our flocks be without water to drink."

"And abandon your three daughters?" Deborah asked. "If God were to strike you dead, would He not be killing us ever so surely?"

"What does it matter? My lineage will be no more without a son. A man will take you for his wife and so, too, your sisters. I have sacrificed the finest unspotted sheep in the herd so that the Lord God would open the heavens and give us rain, even until forty days and forty nights if it be so, to water the parched soil and bring back to life our dying crops. And what has that brought us?"

"The Lord God will be merciful," Deborah said, touching her hand to her father's shoulder. "He will provide."

"He will not provide," Zilpar said. "And so it is that I curse him!"

"The penalty for such words is to be put to death!" she said, tears streaming from her eyes.

Zilpar looked at his daughter with the bared teeth of a wild animal. "Would that I be granted such a mercy!"

"Father, no!" Deborah moved to her father and tried to embrace him. But he tossed her to the ground.

"Would that you had been a son!" he yelled, bending down and pointing a finger in her face. He rose, then spat upon her feet. "You were but my very first curse. Would that you had been my last."

Lashem could stand no more. He knew that by custom Zilpar could treat his own daughter this way. He could treat her in almost any way possible for she was nothing more than a daughter. That was the law.

But even so, Lashem could bear it no more. His heart ached for this woman. He knew he could love her. He could not—

Had he just said within his mind an unspoken thought that he believed he could love her? A woman he had met but hours ago?

Yes, he had. And that had been right. His heart had quickened from the moment he saw her. And he thought he had seen in her eyes, and in the laughter at his jest, that she had felt something in her own heart for him.

And so he broke every custom of hospitality he had ever been taught.

"Leave her alone!" he commanded.

Zilpar whirled upon him, eyes wide. He grasped hold of Lashem's garments, teeth barred, and breath filled with the stench of decaying animals. "What did you say to me? What did you dare say to the host who has taken you into his care?"

"I said to leave her alone!" Lashem said. "And curse not the Lord God Jehovah, the God of our fathers."

"I'll curse whomever I please," Zilpar said, a thick wetness dripping down from the corner of this mouth into his ragged beard.

Deborah stood between the two men. "Worry not about me, Lashem," she said. With pleading in her soft brown eyes, she said, "Say not a word about this to any man. If we have earned any favor in your eyes—" Her gaze bore into him. "If *I* have earned any favor in your eyes, speak not a word of this. My father's mind has grown ill and feeble before its time. The evil spirits have come more and more often, sometimes as often as ten times between the fullness of the moon. Their ferocity wounds my soul. But I could not bear for him to be put to death."

Deborah knew it to be immodest for any maiden to be so close to a man who was not her father or brother or husband, and now she understood why. It wasn't just a custom to protect her honor. So many customs felt silly to her, though she dared not speak of it. But there was nothing foolish about this one.

She felt the heat coming off Lashem, a heat that wrapped itself around her as if in the embrace of a husband to a wife.

Her eyes widened. Had she actually thought that? Well, of course she would think immodest thoughts when standing almost up against such a man. Of course, she would think immodest thoughts looking into those brown, protecting eyes.

She felt the heat of a thousand noonday suns rise into her face.

And rise into her loins.

Oh, the shame of it!

And then Lashem spoke the words that silenced father's evil spirit and her own pleas for clemency on his behalf.

"I wish to take Deborah as my wife," he said.

Deborah felt her heart stop and her breath fail her. Her legs weakened and all about her spun wildly, making her think for an instant that her father's madness had now become her own.

But she steadied herself and stared at Lashem, who looked to her for her assent, and smiled at what he saw.

Deborah awaited her father's response, then cried out when she heard it.

"You may not have her!" Zilpar said. "You come into my abode and do not respect my hospitality. Then you try to take away all that I have left! No, you cannot have her. Get out!"

Deborah held her breath.

"If I leave, I will tell others of your curses at the Lord your God," Lashem said.

Deborah wanted to cry out, "No! No! No!" but she could not speak.

"You will be stoned to death, for there will be people who remember me from before I left," Lashem said. "They will know that I serve the Lord God Jehovah and speak no false witness of any man. And they will look at you and your evil spirit will betray you. You will not be able to keep it silent, and all will know of your madness."

Zilpar choked at the words.

"Or you can come with us, as we make a new home for ourselves as husband and wife in the land about Harrar," Lashem said. "You have lived a long, hard life, and we will care for you and your other two daughters until they are wed. There is but one condition. You must never again strike or spit upon your daughter. For she will be my wife, and if you bring her to harm, your life will be forfeited."

Zilpar glared at Lashem.

"And so," Lashem said, "I ask again for your blessing."

When she heard her father's barely whispered assent, Deborah's heart leaped for joy.

She watched her future husband with pride, knowing she had met a man who could handle her unspoken thoughts, and even encourage them. She would not only be a good wife but have a voice for the first time in her life. A smile formed upon her face so wide she was sure it could be seen even through the thickest of veils.

Copyright © 2018 by D. H. Hendrickson.

Brenda Carre's short fiction has appeared in the Magazine of Fantasy and Science Fiction, *in Fiction River Anthologies,* Pulp Literature Magazine *and on BundleRabbit. brendacarre.com. "St. Jean and the Wish" is the sequel to "St. Jean and the Dragon" which appeared in* Fiction River: Alchemy and Steam.

ST. JEAN AND THE WISH

(A Jane and Jinn Mystery)

by Brenda Carre

Jane Watson, a paranormal sleuth is a contemporary of the great Sherlock Holmes, but Jane works in the secret branch of British Intelligence's "Inexplicable Beings" Unit. Her amenuensis, St Jean, is an ages-old Jinni rescued from his bottle on an earlier adventure with poltergeists in the British Museum. Jane and her Jinni have been falling in love ever since.

In this age of iron and steam, the only dragons Jane and I wish the layman to know of are the ones Robert Stevenson and Jackson Churchward have taught to *chuff chuff chuff* into motion. These dragons spout acrid soot from their smokestacks as they fly down iron rails, and the squeals of holiday-bound children in boaters and sailor-suits are screeches of joy, not terror.

Yet, my beautiful sleuth and I know there *are* real dragons in England.

Dragons "sleep" in places the layman least suspects and if the layman were to know of them and all of the other Inexplicable Beings in our world, this could end all order in our Realm.

"Your mess, your mop up," said Lessie (Lestrade) Halsall, our contact in the secret branch known as the Bureau of Inexplicable Events. She'd made the trip from Whitehall to Jane's flat in Kensington to show us the newspaper report that had come from County Durham.

"This is Angharad is it not? This mysterious beast putting paid to whole flocks of sheep by night? I must have you know my dear brother brought this to my attention. Would you have his branch go into this—or, for that matter, the sleuth *he* works with?"

"No. Of course not." Jane folded the newspaper precisely and returned it to Lessie. I noted, however, that her fingers quivered. "It is most likely Angharad, and it is our mess—well, mine if you must have it. St. Jean is merely my assistant. You must now telegraph whoever inhabits the position of Corporate Magistrate up there in Northumbria and inform him that St. Jean and I will meet with him at Durham Cathedral tomorrow afternoon at four."

"And whom do I say you *are?*" said Lessie, lips pursed.

"I shall be Lady Saratoga working on behalf of the tenant farmers of the afflicted county. We must hope to Heavens he does not own a copy of Burke's Peerage. Advise the fellow to bring full details of the Mysterious Disturbance. I need to know if anyone around there has seen Angharad. I must hope that St. Jean and I can find a way to suitably contain our dragon before she is detected. It would be a great shame to kill her."

"Or she us. I could grant you a wish," I murmured, nursing my brandy and looking at the roses on Jane's carpet. "One wish could make the problem of Angharad go away as if it had never happened, and no one the wiser, save for us and the Inexplicables."

Jane sighed. "This is too complex a problem to diffuse with one wish, St. Jean. We'll deal with this, Lessie. Please tell the Inexplicables not to be concerned, and for heaven's sake diffuse any worries your brother Joseph has voiced."

"It's not Joseph who worries me but the brilliant sleuth he works for. If *he* sniffs this out we're sunk," said Lessie as she went out to the hackney she had waiting in the street.

Jane turned to me and straightened my cravat. I had not quite got the knack of tying the thing, as yet. Since the day Jane had pulled me out of my bottle and into her service, my powers had been fading. I was becoming more human and less of a Jinn, and I'd begun to turn to lesser bottles for their mild gift of well-being on those long days we had no case to solve.

"You still want to leave then?" she said to me.

How could I tell her the pull of her world was waxing for me?

No, rather that the pull of *her* was waxing for me. A Jinn feels little in the way of love. That I was feeling this new emotion—it was yet another sign I had to make a choice if Jane did not. "My usefulness fades," I told her instead.

"When we freed Angharad last year, I could still pass through walls as easily as a thief crawls through an open window. I could spy for you in ways a visible assistant could not do. I think the time will come very soon when your wish will no longer be available. I beg you to use it now."

"So, if your powers fade, will that make you less of a Jinn?" she mused, dusting off the front of my waistcoat.

"I do not know. I know of no other than you who so chooses to deny the wish."

"I would not do you harm." She whispered looking up intently at me.

Just the slightest move would take me to her lips. Yet at that moment her valet Mr. Huston attended us with Jane's packed valise. If I could have colored, I would have. "You have one wish—I beg you not waste it."

I nodded to Huston, tossed back my brandy and went to fetch Jane's wrap.

"Thank you, Huston," she nodded going to the portable apothecary she always kept upon the top of her piano. As Huston went to hail a hackney, Jane continued our conversation in the parlor. "The problem is I have always made my own wishes, St. Jean. You *are* still useful. You have centuries—no—you have aeons worth of knowledge inside you I can rely upon."

Ah, yes. Aeons bound up in a silken waistcoat, tails, and superfine trousers.

"An Inexplicable to deal with Inexplicables," I murmured.

"Yes, quite," she beamed at me. I slid the wrap about her shoulders, unable to stop my hands from lightly caressing her upper arms as I placed it around her, my touch lingering until she looked up with eyes warmed with a little more than surprise.

I hastily pulled back, self-conscious, and donned my beaver hat and looked at the ink-haired man with the long side whiskers and perfectly-trimmed mustachio in the reflection across from me. My dark, saturnine face would not have appeared in a mirror even a month ago. It was not the face of a Jinn any more; it was the face of a man who must make a choice. I had the length of this case to make it.

Like the dragon we sought, I would set myself free.

While we waited for Durham's Magistrate to arrive, Jane and I wandered about the great square-towered Cathedral's ancient graveyard, her dove-grey skirts swishing across the grasses. A tranquil place of rest high above the Medieval town, where lay the tomb of St Cuthbert and the sacristy of Bede the Venerable. From our high hill, we admired the vista of green far below us beyond the River Wear.

Jane shaded her keen eyes with a hand. "So where does she sleep, do you think? There are miles of fat farms stretching out there all the way from Sunderland to Berwick-on-Tweed."

"That she still sleeps by day is a good sign. It means she is still torpid," I replied.

"She?" said a voice behind us. He must have come out of the Cathedral.

Jane turned with her gloved hand already extended. "Oh la, sir, you startled me. What have you for me?"

The corpulent, no-neck Magistrate for County Durham was fairly bursting out of his brown tweed waistcoat. Florid of face and bulbous of nose, he took the folio of papers from under his crooked arm and bowed.

"Geordie Leeland, Magistrate for County Durham, Mum—er M'lady Saratoga."

"Yes, yes, let me see."

Jane snatched the folio out of his brown-gloved hand and swiftly scanned the many papers of complaint. "This is Mr. St. Jean, my assistant," she said.

Leeland touched the brim of his beaver.

I returned a curt nod and read the documents over Jane's shoulder, trying not to notice how amazing her hair smelt.

Good to see no mention of Angharad. Yet the tenor was dismaying. They were full of supernatural reference. Taking my cue to be the heavy in this encounter, I took a menacing step toward him. "Surely, Mr. Leeland, the 'broon' man o'the Moors, the Portobello Shape-shifter, Red Caps? These are without substance!"

Leeland quailed away and fawned toward Jane. "Erm, yes, but I can't stress enough tha' well over a thousand sheep ha' gone astray in this past moonth. The tenants are happy to tease themselves into a pleasant tizzy with the *broon man* when all is safe and good, but when summat like this happens, the stories of the Small Folk doon't seem so small. We all now t'is unlikely to be wolves."

Jane tutted. "Of course, not wolves, but not…"

She paused in surprise.

I was half-turned between she and the chunky Magistrate. His back was to the fields beyond the Wear; thus he did not see what we could see: far distant, yet discernable to the naked eye, something huge dipping down from the clouds, claws extended, vast pinions arrowed back as the dragon dropped.

Angharad.

She dove like a falcon the size of a frigate, stooping from the sun-kissed sky, red-gold against the white of a cloud. Beautiful and deadly, she rose with her kill. A white something just visible in her claws. It took less than ten breaths for her to climb high enough to be gone.

The lumpy Magistrate turned to squint at the fields and returned his attention to us. "Loovely prospect out there, tha's certain. Such a pity I don't have my spectacles to mark what you saw."

"You know who I am," said Jane. This was the question rhetorical: a statement of surprised understanding.

You know who I am.

Leeland bowed. Double chins rolling over his stock, Leeland looked down and toed a long patch of grass his brogue.

"Aye. The 'broon' man at your service, mum. As the Corporate Magistrate for the Seelie Folk hereabouts, I speak for all when I say I'm relieved you have come to make terms with Angharad."

"I make terms? What terms? I have been trying to contact your people forever!"

As he looked up, Jane gave him one of those dazzling smiles that made my heart turn over.

"They'll be your terms to make, mum, not ours. You moost keep us out of this. The Small Folk both Seelie and Unseelie are a-feared to disturb yon royal dragon. She's apart from all of us in more ways than one. The Seelie worship her. The Unseelie fear how she did down the Foes of Merlin. Even were she not what she is, all dragons can be flighty beasts. especially the wyrms—no joke being made. All are temperamental. See now…"

He led us over to a quieter place in the graveyard, beside a tall stone that said, *Not all who wander are lost.*

I grinned at the irony, given a sojourn I once made into the future.

Leeland scowled at me, jiggling his folio under his arm.

"Please continue," I said.

He grunted and looked at Jane. "See now—'tis not just dragons are temperamental. The Unseelie are too. If you so mooch as let your Bureau know the Seelie are helping you, there'll be a war among the Small Folk sooch as you don't ever want to see."

"Then what have you for me? Documents only?" asked Jane, disappointed.

He toed the ground again. "As a gift, because you gave Angharad back her soul and set her free from the Foes of Merlin, our lot have given me permission to tell you she sleeps on the Holy Isle."

"Lindisfarne?" breathed Jane.

"Aye, mum. Somewhere about the ruins of the ancient Abbey."

"St. Jean, how far is the Holy Isle?"

"The ruins of Lindisfarne Abbey are approximately 77.9 miles from where we stand now. It would take a swan about two hours to fly there. I could estimate a dragon to take less than that, but not much."

"No getting there before nightfall?"

I shook my head. "Not without a deal of magical assistance."

Jane looked at the Magistrate. He shook his head and his jowls jiggled. "No active assistance from our lot, not even from me, mum. I am none but th' Magistrate of Durham reporting complaints."

I sighed. "Then, if this is the case, Jane, I suggest we take the Rail as far as Lowick, and overnight at the Black Bull Inn. It's no more than an eight-mile ride to Lindisfarne from there. I've been told The Bull provides a tasty board and the best mead in the country."

Jane clutched her wrap a little tighter about her. "Very well. Their hostler can secure us a couple of hacks for the rest of the ride. We'll set out in the morning at a time dependant on the tides. I've no desire to wet my feet whilst being pursued by a dragon."

"Aye, aye, a good choice," said Leeland. "I wish I could coom along and introduce you to the Black Bull himself. He's on our side."

"We know our animal—and she us," said Jane leaning forward from her plush seat so our foreheads nearly touched. We were so close we must have looked like trysting lovers to anyone who cared to take note of us and I can't say that I am at all disappointed by that. I wished it were true—and more.

A pleasing scent of pipe tobacco teased the air. The lamps were lit as we *chuff chuffed* north, casting Jane's lovely reflection against the window glass.

Jane went on. "Angharad is royal, that must count for something—I must hope—no matter how irascible she was the night we freed her. Hopefully she still remembers she granted me a favor. If this be the once and future time we have to meet with her, then we must make it count…"

"Make it count how?" I took her kid-gloved hands in mine to continue the appearance of intimacy between us. My fingers caress her gloved hand, even though—no doubt—that was too indecent in public

She allowed it, yet her surprise was very genuine. There was even the slightest catch in her breath as she explained. "We must make it count by turning Angharad to our side. You heard what Leeland inferred?"

"One does not hear an inference, Jane. One assumes it."

"Yes, yes—well. I assume a great unrest among the Small Folk. I assume the whole of this Island—and possibly the world—sits upon a powder keg of disagreement between Seelie and Unseelie. Boggles, Pukas, Redcaps, Braggs—even worse than these may be on the edge of revolt. We need Angharad's help, St. Jean. And possible even the help of her brother, the Pendrake, if he still exists."

I stroked the back of her kid-gloved hand with my thumb. Was that a quiver of feeling in her response or just her way of putting on appearances?

"How do you imagine we can convince Angharad to help us, let alone another one? What can we offer her—and possibly *him*—in return? The freedom of all the sheep in Britain?"

"Of course not. Do not mock me." Jane took her hands back and put a few more breaths of distance between us. "We dare not give Angharad the freedom of the skies or the ground. We have to deal with this tomorrow or we are truly ruined. You heard what Lessie said. I will not have her brother's branch of Home Office alerted. Lessie's already had enough trouble keeping our doings secret from him."

"As in the Baskerville case," I said.

"Hush!" Jane hissed so loudly people looked our way.

I leaned toward her once more. "You are weary my dear," I said loudly enough for the curious to hear. As if to soothe her ruffled feathers, I stroked a curl of honey hair behind her ear and murmured so people could not hear. "Let's talk about this behind closed doors." My voice, unintended, was also a form of caress. The implication behind my words and actions were a show for those around us, but also filled with truth.

As if to fight the chemistry between us she flared again. "We will not talk about the Baskerville case!"

Frustration bristled. "I do not accept being chided by you, *my dear*. I do not want to be just your "assistant" anymore. You ignored my suggestions in the case of the Baskervilles, and it moved swiftly out of our reach. Fortunately, the real Hounds dwell near Hay-on-Wye and not in Dorset."

As Jane's look of outrage grew and pert face went pink, I forged on with what I had long planned to say. Much of it born of my own heart's frustration.

"As I said, you ignored my warnings with the Baskervilles, and our dealings were nearly uncovered. It took months for our Bureau to conceal what really happened when Angharad awoke. We cannot let this get out of hand. I want an equal partnership, Jane; my decisions holding as much weight as yours. My agreement as well as yours."

"This is *my* department, St. Jean. I developed it. I recruited Lessie and all who support me. I have the training. You are *bound* to me."

I tried not to let her words hurt me. I thought I meant more to her. "I am *not* bound to you," I said through gritted teeth. "A pity I did not stress that earlier. My wish is bound to you, nothing more. My inclinations are my own. And, if anything, you might call me as Seelie as the 'broon man'. Not that my nature has meant much to you to this point."

"And if I ignore your wishes?" she said, also through her teeth.

"Then what concerns the Seelie and the Unseelie will be but one unrest you need to contain," I said, as our train *chuffed* into the station and the conductor's whistle blew.

Jane was silent in the musty carriage—her manner as stiff as if I had stepped on her toes. She remained so at the Black Bull as the earnest porter took our valises up to our rooms—my room merely engaged for appearances now I was visible.

"I need nothing more tonight than to put down my head," Jane said and went immediately up the oaken stair. The stiffness of her spine said otherwise.

I felt no qualms. I did hope she would sleep. I had no desire to have her wake tomorrow still cranky.

I spent the early hours at over food and spirits, sipping Lindisfarne mead and squirreling away whatever local tittle-tattle our burly host chose to speak of. The mead went down easily. So did a fulsome serving of Steak and Guinness Tart. Eating food was a pleasure I had just begun to experience.

With a mind full of folk tales and a body pleasingly torpid, I went for a walk choosing a distant haystack as my destination in the otherwise flat farmland.

The tiny village slumbered around me. The windows of the Bull were all dark. If Jane was still mulling over the choices I'd given her, the windows disclosed nothing of that. I turned over a few possibilities for the morrow's meeting with Angharad, given she made an appearance at all.

A stile took me into the field, and along a footpath, the scent of a clear night fragrant hay and bright stars over me. "I have to stand by my choice," I said to those fields.

"What choice?" said the haystack now looming in front of me.

"Angharad?" I gasped, backing up fast.

"The same," she replied. Obligingly a pair of slit golden eyes unlidded as Angharad stretched her horned head out of the feathery huddle of wings and tail she had wrapped around herself. Her wings were more swanlike than those of a bat and her three horns more of a spiral than tusk. No cat could have uncoiled from a mound of rumpled fur with more grace.

Angharad flexed one great forepaw, exposed her claws, stretched them out in a wicked array with a gusty sigh. A sharp pink tongue flicked over her teeth and withdrew back into her jaws. A gust of warm breath that smelled of dry grass and sheep's wool enfolded me.

"What choice do you speak of St. Jean? Did you know you were speaking aloud? As you gain a man's body, you also seem prone to the obtuseness that goes with mankind."

"Obtuseness?" I said.

Angharad rumbled. "It means insensitive. Not sharp. Even dim-witted, given you have such a brilliant mind. Come forward, man. My business tonight is wholly with you. If you accept what I have to say, then I may choose not to kill you tomorrow."

She rumbled again.

I read this rumble as laughter. I approached her warily nonetheless as she rolled onto her side revealing her glorious mailed belly.

"Ahh." Her horns gouged grooves in the grass as she scratched them. She stretched until I heard her joints crack. "I heard what you said on your noisy amble over here in the fresh air. What interested me was not what you see—obtuse man—but your desire to be respected. No less than what your Jane must want from you. Respect without reserve."

Was I dreaming, or was I having a philosophical discussion with a dragon about my relationship with Jane? "I do respect her. I demanded a partnership," I said.

"Ah? A partnership? *Demanded* is it? Without any kind of agreement given? Is this how you plan to approach *me* tomorrow on the Holy Isle? Is this how you hope to fight the wyrms when they arise?"

The dragon's great spiked tail thumped down between us.

I staggered back with a yelp. She gave a deep-throated purr. "Your Jane is a woman, but she has the spirit of a dragon. Go back, sir, and think on this. You cannot contain me, nor can you contain her. You must find a better way if you hope for—*hmmm*—a partnership."

Angharad rumbled again.

"What better way?" I said.

"Set her free, you idiot. I spent time enough in that hovel in Cornwall to know what being trapped feels like. You must trust your Jane as you trust your own soul. Your threats were base and baseless. You cannot leave her, and you know it and not just because you love her. You must remain her contact with the Small Folk, and as such you must continue to be Seelie. How you will do that as you become more human, I cannot say. Now go away, St. Jean. Your heart is showing. You have drunk enough tonight."

"Drunk? I do not suffer from dri…" I began as the ground crashed up to meet me.

I woke in that field as the rooster began to crow. In my head was a terrible grinding of knives. A gnashing of teeth could not begin to describe it. In my stomach was an ominous turmoil I never wished to experience again. I'd drunk far too much. I got to my feet still reeling. Had I been dreaming?

No. Though the field of last night stretched out in many directions with nary a haystack upon it, in front of me were a triple set of gouges that carved through the grass and into rich soil—and a memory too—something that Angharad had said: *Is this how you hope to fight the wyrms when they rise?*

I grabbed my face in my hand and groaned. "Ohh—I am such an idiot—a bottle-soused idiot!"

Given the height of the sun, it was already well into morning. If I knew my Jane, she'd have left without me.

Yet Jane had *not* left, much to my great delight. Our hacks were saddled in the stable yard. I stumbled through the open Dutch doorway into the common room. Jane was there tapping her toe, dressed in her best grey gown, her velvet pelisse over it against the windy day, a fetching bonnet on hair done up in a business-like bun. Jane took one look at my face and unlatched her apothecary.

"A mug of ale!" she demanded of our host who hastened to pour it. When the drink came, she poured white powders into it which immediately co-mingled and added a fiz.

"Drink, Idiot," she snapped, though I detected some worried affection in the rebuke.

"What did you think you were about?" she asked a time later, once we were on our way and my brain had stopped thumping against my skull. I thought of what Angharad had said to me the night before, and thus I answered truthfully, holding nothing back.

"I was thinking about how to make some sense of living outside my bottle—without giving a thought to what 'living' means—or dying for that matter. I have never had to concern myself with that before. I was immortal. Before today, all I concerned myself with was your death, Jane. Protecting you. Now I know one wish is not enough. I have come to realize

I am an idiot to think so. I had to become drunk to understand that."

I looked at her and saw her lovely face go still. She didn't respond, but I saw the stiffness in her spine now was for the ride and not for me. As we took to the tidal flats and crossed the narrow causeway between Lindisfarne Isle and the coast of Great Britain, I told Jane what the dragon had said last night of the wyrms. I told her that the dragon planned to speak to her alone—that what would take place was not for me. That my instruction had happened last night but that I would help in any capacity I could.

"I am at your service Jane. No matter what I said last night, I beg your forgiveness. Angharad called me an obtuse idiot, and so I am."

Jane spluttered with laughter. "I begin to think you were right about getting drunk, St. Jean. It has done for you what a great deal of cold sense has not. Did the ale and my powders help?"

"Immensely," I grinned as we sloshed to the shore. "We have little time now to meet with your dragon though. We have a few hours at most to negotiate her assistance until the tide turns again to open the causeway."

"St. Jean?" I turned to look back at the way now already inundated by the incoming waters of the North Sea.

"St. Jean, we're in trouble. There are pilgrims on the road ahead…"

We were in trouble, but Pilgrims were the least of our concerns. The two Sea-Wyrms rising up from the waves between us and the mainland were, and they were swimming towards us as fast as a tidal bore and as loud as the rattle of storm surf on shingle.

Instead of running away, my terrified hack plunged towards them. Bucking like a fiend, he threw me off into waist-high sea. Coming up choking, I saw the nearest worm take my hack in merciless jaws and before I spit out the sea and had a chance to gasp my lungs full of air, both my horse and the wyrm were gone beneath the waves. I stumbled in panic toward the land my every sense alive to the noise of the second wyrm coming after me now.

My mortality hit me like a fist. I had seriously thought my greatest wish was to become human and spend the rest of my humanity with Jane. It was not. I didn't want to die. Pure and simple and it was over before I could even grasp how sweet life might be.

I fell gasping to my hands in the water, my face smacking the salty waves as the other wyrm came at me. I heard Jane scream. I heard the distant screams of the Pilgrims too upon the holy road. Time slowed for me to the pace of a snail to the drumming of her hack's hooves trying in vain to save me. All our plans were done, for now, to deal with Angharad secretly.

In fact, to deal at all.

"Vanish!" I heard her shriek. "My wish! I wish the wyrms to vanish! Be gone!"

Struggling to my feet, I saw her coming, her bonnet gone, salt spray flying. Her horse soaked to his flanks. I saw her despair as she understood her wish had failed. She had waited too long to claim it.

But she had tried! Oh, mortality. She had tried.

"St. Jean, get out of the way," she screamed driving her terrified horse between the oncoming wyrm and me. It was a wicked, silvery beast, all body, no wings at all, and it twisted at me through the water like an eel. Its teeth were needles the length of railroad spikes and its maw an open cavern.

"Mortality," I roared at the wyrm. "Take me, you bastard—not her, not them. I am Seelie!"

So, this is death, I thought, as the monster ignored Jane and the pilgrims on their mounts. I smelled its raw fishy breath. I felt its great teeth pass through me, and yet I felt no pain. The whole of Jane's world blurred and faded and I was gone out of it. The wyrm swallowed me down. I found myself stood in a cavern—like Jonah in the belly of a whale.

Alive? Dead? I didn't know.

Above me were great stalactites of crystal and limestone and beneath me the cavern's tongue. The heart of the dragon.

"Halfway between mortal and Jinn, he could not yet kill you. That was nicely done, St. Jean, *bach*. It was you who used that wish, not she."

"Who are you?" I said.

Again, the great voice rumbled about me—a voice with a decided Welsh accent. "I am the Pendrake, the brother of Angharad, the spirit of this land who has always dwelt beneath the stone save for one time long ago when I fought with my sister for the right to save Arthur. My likeness still lies upon the flag of Wales."

"Am I dead then, Pendrake? And where are you?"

"I am here, beneath the ground. The Wyrms are illusions created by me. The one that swallowed you was a doorway, a kind of portal to bring you to me. You should know about portals, as you lived in that bottle for so very long."

"Does the wyrm still threaten my Jane?"

"*Your Jane*, now is it? Well, well, A long way you have come to knowing that? No, brave one. Dead, she is not. I tell you, *bach*, you took on yourself to use that wish in the spirit of guard and self-sacrifice, knowing you were becoming mortal. Never have I seen one of your fey folk do this, not in my own long years of being. On this day you were halfway between two realms, the immortal realm and the mortal. You are also between the realms of the fey. You are both Seelie and Unseelie, for what is a Jinn, but both? In your taking on your destiny, you shouted your mortality into the face of that wyrm. You did not know he was an illusion created by me. What you did, you did for courage and love, and I can admire this. I took you to me for that. You are now under stone. Your Jane lives above, *bach*, and goes to talk with my sister."

Thank God. If I had given all to save Jane that was worth something. "What of the Pilgrims?"

Pendrake gave a soft rumble. "Ach, they stand upon the Holy Isle, those pilgrims. What better place for a holy experience, is it? Today they will have seen a true St. George vanquish a dragon and think naught of it but that they had a holy vision. Your Jane will surely see to that."

"St George?" I said.

"Of a sort, *bach*—my dear friend. Come forward."

The cavern narrowed as though into a creature's gullet. I had to stoop to get through this throat. It was dark at first, yet soon it widened into the vault where the Pendragon lay. Here the heat was greater. My boots smoked and dried on the floor. The great dragon's body was a fiery red-gold. Spines of horn stood up all along his rugged back almost like flames dancing. His huge bat-wings were spiked at the joints, his paws mailed in red armor and his claws like scimitars as long as a man's arm. The Pendrake's front fangs over-shot his pebbled jaws—long enough to grip and tear a body apart with Unseelie abandon. He was prone, his lids hooded over slits half seen but there was power there—enough to explode into action should the need come.

"The Seelie and the Unseelie both fear you," I said, recognizing that here before me lay the spirit of this Kingdom.

"All the fey powers of this island do fear that I break free, St. Jean, *bach*. I hope it be not so, for should I need to come forth it will be with fire and molten rock. I am content to rest here. Your Jane is, even now, negotiating a charter with my sister Angharad—secretly, of course. She might be seen only to be contemplating a golden hill of hay out in the quiet fields. The pilgrims now talk about their vision in the ruins of Lindisfarne Abbey far above us."

"You know this how?" I asked, keeping a respectful distance.

"We are close, my sister and I. Through Angharad's dreams, the ground itself tells me all. For me, I am content to sleep and dream the eons away. My sister now belongs above the ground with her feathery wings. This is her time to bring peace among the Small Folk. Do not begrudge her the sheep or the seals she chooses by night and the hunting she must do out of sight and mind. It will be her task to keep the Seelie and the Unseelie from war. I appoint you and Jane now to make it your task to be her Anti-heralds."

"Anti-heralds?" I said.

The Pendrake bared his fangs in a cavernous grin. "From now on, you and your Jane will be told by one of the Small Folk where Angharad is and what she is about. It will then be your task, yours and Jane's, to draw the eye of the world elsewhere. You must do this with care so that you also draw the eyes of that 'other' sleuth who is so much Jane's rival for attention. Prick his interest, if you so desire. Be his goad to excellence, but always and ever draw his eye from us.

"You must operate carefully by making *him* famous. The less this world knows of you, the better off it shall be. Will you do this for us, St. Jean, *bach*?"

I went to one very dirty wet knee on the cavern floor before him. My knee steamed from the contact and small diamonds stuck to the weave of my trousers. (Diamonds Jane and I later made use of….) "I will do as you ask, Sire, with all that lies in me as both a Jinn and a man."

"Very good, St. Jean. So the world is often saved by un-seen heroes. As both genius and man, I shall make you my contact between the Seelie and the Unseelie. Use it carefully. Through you, your Jane shall know where next your journeys take you. Be gone now, *bach*—I am sleepy."

"Erm, be gone *how*, Sire?" I asked.

"You entered through the maw of a wyrm, did you not? The portal of the wyrm can take you out again. I will set you free, but only in part. I may call you back again as I desire." The Pendrake gave a mighty yawn and those cavernous jaws opened wide, each fang long enough to impale me.

"Oh Mortality," I breathed and stepped into his mouth.

"St. Jean?"

I turned at the breathless voice behind me. Turned away from wind off the causeway, a wind now harsh on drenched clothing—icy flesh, my hat long lost to the waves, the suck of the water squelching inside my boots. The sand of the beach sharing place in my breast pocket with the Pendrake's diamonds. Who knew how cold the North Sea was, how far the shore, how deeply my muscles ached and how frantic now beat the heart within me?

"Jane!" I said.

I gave her no chance to dismount before I was there, reaching up to haul her down from her horse, pulling her into me, her arms frantic around me, mine hard around her, her mouth on mine. *At last. Oh, at last.*

She felt amazing. Vibrant. Alive. The kiss went on and on, until even my own half-mortal form dictated a need for air. I reluctantly pulled my lips from hers, dipping in again to nip her bottom lip and make her gasp before completely retreating.

"Do you still want me to be bound to you?" I asked her, my voice husky with need and happiness welling.

She blinked up at me, still in a euphotic stunned haze from our kiss. "I shouldn't have said that. I was just feeli—"

"I know: hurt. So was I." I slid my arms tighter around her waist, pulling her close again. "I wasn't meaning being bound to you as a Jinn. I mean being your partner. Not only in our work, but in life, too. In love."

"Yes," she all but breathed, warmth and excitement in her eyes.

I leaned in to kiss her again, only to be shoved back, playfully.

"You're soppy wet—oh lord, St. Jean!"

"Oh, Mortality—oh, Sweet Mortality," I sighed into her loose hair.

This moment was priceless; a gift, not a wish. Like the diamonds I would soon place about her finger.

Rei Rosenquist is a queer agender (they/them) speculative and contemporary fiction writer who depicts a wide variety of identities struggling to find a place in a wide variety of worlds. They are also a lifelong barista, baker, and nomad. Over the years, they have traveled to many countries, engaged many peoples, picked up new habits, and learned new languages. But, some things never change. For them, the constants of life are made up of love stories, great coffee, delicious food, and traveling. Rei's work can be found in Enter the Aftermath *by TANSTAAFL Press,* Beauty & Wickedness *by Blackbird Publishing, and* Midwinter Fae *by Blackbird Publishing. You can also find more of Rei's work by visiting their website reirosenquist.com. Stay in touch by connecting via Facebook (Rei Rosenquist), Instagram (@rylrosenquist) and Twitter (@rylrosenquist).*

THE HEART FINDS THE WAY

by Rei Rosenquist

This is the night I will never forget.

The world is in the fullness of summer, bathed in a rich golden light that alights like butterflies, gentle on my sun-speckled skin. The air is pregnant with the smell of mature wheat grass, a heady mixture of sweet and earthy. The sky, bottle blue and clear, hangs low like a sheet overhead, heavy with humidity. The taste of woodsmoke is on the tip of my tongue from the distant fires of cooks preparing for the night market's festivities.

Everything is perfect.

I'm sitting on a hill, covered in long thin white whipper flowers that smell like hay when it goes to seed, as it is now. There are already small housemade fireworks going off all around the low ring of hills that surround the town I've grown up in. The sun, just about to set, still warms the back of my work-worn neck. A breeze plays with the downy tendrils of wayward hair that broke free from my thick carrot-orange braid. Cast before me, my own shadow makes a long line across the hill, marking the end of day. I look at the outline of myself, feeling strangely huge. As if something bigger than me is standing atop both my shoulders.

A vision takes hold of me. My hand in someone else's. Me and this companion stand in utter darkness, but we are unafraid. Something rises into the air, and together, we disappear.

What a strange vision.

I'd never leave my people like that. A heavy feeling of loneliness fills me up, as if proving me wrong. I push the vision away from my memory as suddenly as it came by, telling myself it's just another silly daydream. No time for that right now. I need to get back into town before the festivities begin.

I stand, stretching my back, and then reach a hand into the small silk pouch wrapped around my belly. I pull out three cloudy grey-blue triangles. I spread my palm wide, and the gems catch the last rays of sunlight and sparkle, spitting rainbows across the green. I roll the gems happily between my dirty fingers, thinking what kind of treasures I'll buy at night market tonight. Perhaps a new belly pouch or a bigger shoulder satchel. Maybe, even, a roomy travel pack. I've always wanted to go on long treks into the distant woods, only my birthing pair, Weavebreak and Moonshade, say I'm not old enough yet for such arduous solo adventures.

I think they're scared.

Their Third-Hand disappeared many moons ago, leaving just the two of them to tend our little family alone. Nobody actually knew where White Fur went. We tell high tales of the critical missions White Fur must be on, called as ze were by the deities of this world to banish some great darkness from the lands. Only, I suspect Weavebreak and Moonshade don't believe any of that. It only makes for a better story, and that makes us all feel better.

The truth of the matter is most likely much sadder and simpler. An accident in the forest. A slip down a long slide and a broken leg. Or, more gruesome, a sneak attack by a pack of starved wolfbane after the drought that year. Looking for a meal. And a small, compact Third-Hand like White Fur would have been easy to pick off.

I breathe out, sagging, when I hear footsteps on the grass.

"Are those sky gems, Shadow?" asks a voice behind me.

I turn and see the speaker leaning against a small tree.

"Tiller," I say and smile, tucking my gems away. "You are a sight for a heavy mind."

Tiller is my best friend in all the universe.

We met when our generation was separated according to sex. Carriers on the left, Helpers on the right, and Third-Hands in the middle. Tiller and I had been the only two standing short and thin between the sturdy and stout carriers and the tall, strong-armed helpers. But, it was more than our sex that drove us together. That had just been the first hint that we'd get along. We stayed together because of everything else. We fit, somehow. Like two tiny little matching puzzle pieces missing from the middle of a perfect painting.

"How'd you know I was up here?" I ask, already knowing the answer.

"You always come up here before a night market and festival celebration," Tiller says.

It's true. I do. Tiller knows me that well.

I find myself soaking up the sight of my old familiar friend with a new kind of excitement. Like drinking down sweet river water after a long drought. Orange locks that match mine but today look more like sunrise rays than hair. And Tiller's freckles across zer wide flat nose look like comet dust spraying across zer golden face of a sky. Zer skin, halfshade paler than mine, is like a living iteration of wood gold, whereas I look like wet mud flecked with toasted wheat chaff. And then, there's Tiller's most distinct feature—zer soft purple eyes. Today, I see layered nimbus clouds touched by the dying rays of the departing sun.

"You going to night market with your gems?" Tiller asks, eying my belly pack.

"Sure am," I beam. "Want to come with me?"

"If you help me carry these," Tiller says and holds out two large bundles of sticks.

Tiller's family uses these sticks to make the special sugar crystal festival treats. Tiller's family has been in the food business for over two hundred starcycles, which is longer than anyone has been in any business in the whole town. Tiller's birthing pair-Flint and Fan-claim that their family goes even further back than a mere two hundred star-cycles when the town was first formed. They say Tiller's family has been in the food-making line of work since before the mountains even formed this valley.

Nobody believes them, of course. But, like all our stories, it's fun to hear and retell wild tales of the spirits who came before us. Those great beings who walked through forests that no longer exist, creating streams of pure wood gold, running with bright purple eye geodes like they were water. Wandering among trees with bark darker than the night sky, standing taller than long houses swaying in breezes full of a warm, gentle white fog. Sharing their visions openly like words or song amongst themselves.

That's why we vision, the legends go. Because we are still connected to the great spirits, and to the past.

Some of us, like me, get stronger visions than others. Most of the time, the visions are beautiful but strange. At rare times like today, they are unnerving, and I push them away. Last night, I had a vision that was terrifying.

In it, all I saw was the sky. Black as hardened earth-blood, not a single star light. Not even far off. Just black, thick darkness as far as the mind could reach. That vision made me hurt inside. Like my heart was breaking, cracking open wide, and I didn't even know why.

Only that everything was wrong, and somehow, I had to find a way to fix it.

"Why don't you buy me something, since you're so rich," Tiller jests, bringing me back to the present.

I scrunch up my face. "Sure. I'll buy you ten sticks of rock candy."

"Deal."

We slap our skinny, narrow-fingered hands together with a soft fap like we do when we think we're being funny. This joke of me buying Tiller something ze don't need? It's hilarious. Nobody ever agrees with us, and that's what makes us best friends.

We get each other when no one else does.

"You want to head in?" I ask, pointing down to the town.

"Not yet. I want to wait until dark here, alone with you."

I smile, beaming at Tiller like this moment is a secret. A quiet unspoken spell, just the two of us sitting here until the dark fingers of night cling to the edges of our clothes. I don't know why, but I want it to be. Just us. Alone. Up here on this hill in the grass until the end of day.

Tiller beams back at me and I wonder–is ze feeling the same thing? This sudden private desire to be alone? And if so, what does that mean?

Could we get in trouble for feeling this way?

It doesn't matter. We're here together outside of town, and that's what counts.

We sit together, sides touching in the cooling grass as the rest of the day fades, and the clouds turn colors. Orange and pink and turquoise and that same powdery purple of Tiller's eyes.

I can't help but gaze back and forth, from the sky to Tiller's eyes. Our shoulders press together, warm against the coming night. I breathe in deep and smell that familiar faint smell of cooking sugar, caramel and milk. I lay my head against Tiller's shoulder with a sigh, and we chuckle in unison because we both know Tiller's sharp bone is going straight into my earlobe.

The sound of our laughter is like oil poured over my whole body, filling me to the brim with happiness. I feel more at ease than I have in a long time. Safe and sound. Like nothing could go wrong in all the universe.

Our eyes meet-turquoise green-blue to sky-dusted lavender, and both of our cheeks color. We both look away as quick as we can. I'm looking for words, something to fill the air between us with anything but a confession of how I feel. I hear Tiller start and stop after an intake of breath, facing the same struggle.

I turn, and we accidentally share another look. Both our cheeks color more. I turn away again, chin to my chest. A complicated mixture of joy and anxiety, guilt and giddiness mixes into a noxious chemical in my belly. I can see my hand shaking as I reach for Tiller's elbow.

The problem here is we're both Third-Hands. And, we know that we'll never join hands under the birthing tree, never pick a joint seed, never live together unified under the same familial roof.

We know that, have always known that. And yet….

"The heart goes where it will," my receiver Moonshade always says.

Only how would I get through life if my heart only went where it shouldn't go?

Was this why White Fur was gone? Had zer heart had gone somewhere it shouldn't have gone, like mine was heading now? Someplace outside of our society. Somewhere into the dark unknown forest of love, forbidden. Two Third-Hands falling for one another and disregarding the whole triad of family structure was just not done.

A proper healthy family is this: a Receiver, a Giver, a Third-Hand, and their mutual children. That's how it has always been. That's how it needs to be.

Is this the medicinal fireweed and blue-bark mash that would help that nasty tincture go down? The difficult, bitter, hard-to-swallow truth that White Fur hadn't loved my family, but another Third-Hand? That ze weren't dead, but we had been abandoned?

If that's true, then what exactly did my birthing pair's wisdom mean? How is "the heart going where it will" a good thing? Or, had that bit of wisdom been sarcasm? A bitter lesson in the heart's cruelty?

And why don't I know the answer to any of these questions? Why is it never talked about? For me to feel what I feel must mean surely it has happened before.

I need to ask Tiller if this. If ze also thinks we are becoming…what? What would we be called? We would not be a birthing pair. We would not be a traditional family unit-that involves three. Only, I'm scared to ask. Terrified. Not that I'll be wrong, but that I'm right. That we've fallen into the forbidden territory of same-sex love.

Oh, broken fingers, no.

I turn and see Tiller's mouth partially open, just like mine. We both breathe in to speak words we might forever regret-

And that's when the earth trembles.

Nothing huge like the shaker-breaker that tears down walls and slips roofs open wide. No, this is just a little hiccuping roll of the land. But it's enough to rumble the rocks under our legs and buck Tiller and I away from each other.

"You feel that?" Tiller asks.

"We should warn the town," I say.

"You're right," Tiller agrees.

We stand and move away from one another. We pick our way down the hill slowly. And as we meander, I can tell we're both feeling it-the dread of having to address what just happened. We stay silent all the way into the center of town.

When we arrive, everything looks completely normal.

The townspeople have gathered their wares, set up their vending tents and are busy perusing the aisles of each other's goods while dressed in their fanciest attire. Headdresses full of colorful streamers, long robes with ornate stitch patterns. Lace in complicated weaves decorating sleeves and hems of long skirts. Carved and burn-worked staffs with full pictures of forests, animals from distant lands, and scenes of festivals past. Hats bearing bundles of flowers. Shoes made from woven grass. The occasional antler helmet or cured fur pelt from animals found dead near the outskirts. All manner of personal expressions are present, and the sight is always a joy to me.

I approach the bakers' tent, the smell of yeast and toast greeting me warmly.

"Friends," I address the bakers behind their beautiful aged wood counter.

"A loaf for the festival?" the small, slight Third-hand of the family addresses me back.

"Did you feel the tremble?" I ask in a rush.

The Third-hand is joined by the Giver who smiles at me wanly. "Aren't you a little too old for such pranks?" she admonishes me.

"No joke," I say, frowning, forgetting my manners.

At the mouth of the stone oven, the Receiver gives me a sharp snort. Narrowed eyes and a wrinkled nose say I'm not amusing.

"But—" I start.

"Run along, now," the Receiver says gruffly.

Accepting defeat, I try another cart to the same effect. I run into Tiller on my way to a third cart, who's furrowed forehead says ze have had about as much success as me. We sigh, leaning together in defeat.

"What now?" Tiller asks.

I watch each passing face, noting how not a single mouth speaks about the mini-shaker we'd felt. We need to get everyone's attention collectively. Like a town crier, only more impressive. Something that will shake people up. Something big and loud, but not alarming. We don't want to create panic, after all. Just get people's attention.

A brightly dressed dancer crosses our path to the sounds of oohs and ahhs from the carts and booths. That's it! I look to Tiller who also follows the dancer with zer eyes, turns back to me, and nods. I give Tiller one of our secret signs, two fingers pressed against my opposite palm. Saying: let's use our drama skills to get their attention.

Tiller gives me back a different secret sign: one finger tapping the space between zer eyebrows. Saying: good thinking.

We always speak to each other like this. In hand gestures and secret symbols. With all the time we've spent together, we probably have an entire lexicon of signs and codes between us. A whole language, even.

One that will turn irrelevant as soon as we are matched with our different birthing pairs.

A deadline which will come at the end of this star-cycle.

Three more moons we have left to live in our childhood fantasy world until adulthood is thrust upon us.

Our eyes meet again, only this time I see the same reddening around the edges of Tiller's eyes right before I feel it around mine. The sting of tears bite at my eyelids. I dash them away as quick as I can, acting like there's some dust or pollen bothering me.

Our eyes catch through cracks in our fingers as Tiller is doing exactly the same thing.

Again, we both color and turn away.

"My fellows, my folk, my kin!" I call, throwing my hands in the air and speaking in my best stage voice.

Everyone in their stalls pauses. Those walking beside me turn and cock their heads.

"Tiller and I were just up on the hill there," I say.

Tiller turns in a sweeping motion and points dramatically to the hill where we'd been sitting just outside of town. We simultaneously assume a wide stance, elbows out.

The crowd waits, oddly quiet and captivated by our voices. Oddly reverent. As if we're not just two unmatched kids putting on a show. As if we have something of great import to share. Their attention more rapt than if even the Council of Elders were addressing them.

Strange. Very strange.

I feel a shudder of fear as the darkness of my vision swoops in on me, but I push it away as strongly as I can. That tremor we felt was real, not a vision. And, it could be dangerous.

"And lo! We felt a tremble! A small quake, yes, but you never know! Prepare yourself for a shaker, anyway!" I say like like I'm some kind of official town guard or disaster ward.

The crowd stops, eyes wide, suddenly dark and serious.

"Prepare yourselves," Tiller calls, less dramatic than I.

The crowd hums and nods. Some cheer and some gasp. A few clap. But everyone turns to their family tents and carts, preparing for a storm. I'm stunned into silence. Tiller beside me, equally still.

After a long pause, Tiller nods. "We did our best," ze say.

I nod in agreement.

Maybe that tremble was the preamble to something big. Maybe, it was nothing. But, we did all we could. We shared what we knew. And with that, we join hands and stride on into the night market, ready to lighten our moods with some fun.

Only, I'm too distracted by the feeling of Tiller's hand in mine to concentrate on anything. Because against the silence and the strange shock of something bad coming, Tiller's hand is a boon. A safe harbor. Something I know without question I can cling to.

And that feels both bigger than it ever did and also…strange too.

Like I'm in love with my old familiar friend. I don't know what to do with that thought. And, from the way Tiller is ambling just as aimless as me, it sure seems like ze feel it too. This warm, excited buzzing between us, like energy is charging up my arm and filling up my chest from the feeling of Tiller's skin against mine. I can feel my whole face turn hot, and I don't know what to do to hide it.

"Hey ho!" a high Receiver's voice calls from behind us.

Both Tiller and I stop and turn.

It's Tan standing by the machinists' tent. Tan-an unmatched Giver the same age as us-beckons us over with a long, strong Giver's arm. In stature, Tan is like all Givers. Tall with a muscular frame that grows strong quick. Only, unlike most Givers, Tan is also known for having wide Receiver's hips and thick sturdy Receiver's legs. Her voice is higher than normal, too.

Even Tan's complexion is mixed; part golden brown and part deep earth black, mottled like stone across her sharply angled face. Her shaved head only shows the hints of silver hair that once grew in long swooping rivers. The elders asked she cut it all off since her matching-cycle is coming (like ours). The elders also recommended she start wearing long flowing robes to try and hide the unfit parts of her Giver's body.

I think she looks weighed down in all those beige robes, though.

Both Tiller and I like Tan a lot, regardless of how others feel about her. We're all three different from the norm, and that makes us the same. We don't quite fit in, and that's a kind of fitting in itself. Like the three of us were friends before we even got to know each other.

Probably not true, but like my birthing pair always say, "The heart goes where it wants."

Like White Fur leaving us, I recall again.

Oh, come on. This is night market! Can't I have a little fun instead of thinking about dark and sad stuff? I huff at myself and push the sad thought aside, focusing back on Tan. I wave and smile, heading closer. Tiller takes my lead and comes along, stride for equal stride, like we always go.

"Well, if it isn't the double-thirds," Tan says with a wink.

Tiller and I don't take offense. Instead, we smile and chuckle. Everyone calls us that since we can't be separated but to sleep in our own beds at night. And if it were up to us, even that would change.

I feel a hot rush in my belly at the thought. A prickling of goosebumps at the image of sleeping next to Tiller. I bite my lip to try and hide my reaction. Tiller gives me side-eye, and I look away.

"Say, you two want to see my new air cruiser? My parents just redesigned it for long distance travel,"

"Long distance?" Tiller asks with a chuckle. "What for?"

People in this town never go very far away. We keep to our family trades, our fields, our rivers and streams. We tend our houses and we keep the town going. Nobody travels to the distant mountains or forests.

Nobody but White Fur's legend. Which is just a story because we can't bring ourselves to say what really must have happened. I frown, kicking a rock. My head's full of weird thoughts today. Must be the festival. Night Market always winds me up.

"Let's go see it," I say, just to move my mouth.

"Yes!" Tan exclaims and punches the air in victory.

Tiller and I give each other a smile, both finding Tan's enthusiasm cute. Like we're star-cycles older

and happy to entertain Tan's young talent. I feel a slight blush coming on, but it's easily batted away. Nothing like my feelings for Tiller…which is a funny thing to think. Since when did my feelings for Tiller become associated to blushing and thinking someone's cute?

Anyway.

Tan goes behind a curtain, then flips it back and wheels out an impressive contraption. It's got long wings and two sitting slots. One with a wheel and one with a rudder.

"It's very much like a river boat," Tan explains, shifting the rudder. "Only it uses air instead of water."

"That's amazing!" I gasp, dazzled by the ingenuity of the machine. It looks surprisingly easy to understand.

"Can we give it a whirl?" Tiller asks, just as excited as I feel.

Tan hesitates.

"I'm sure it's too fragile," I say, trying to give Tan an easy out. Probably, Tan's family doesn't want us playing around on something so exquisite, and Tan doesn't want to make us feel like kids by saying so.

"No, it's not that," Tan says, rejecting my peace offering.

I cock an eyebrow, confused. "No?"

"No, it just takes a very specific key to get the cruiser going."

"What's it need?" Tiller asks, curious and excited.

"Three sky gems, all the same size. Don't ask me why, but Dig said she had a vision in which-"

"I have them!" I interrupt, pulling my gems out of my pouch. "Right here."

"Well, I'll be blasted. What are the odds," Tan says, scratching her bald head. "Ok. You two get in. I'll show you how it works."

Tiller and I climb aboard, I into the steering seat and Tiller into the rudder position. And, just as Tan is finished describing how the controls work, someone cheers loudly in the center of the town square. Whoops and cries of excitement rise from all around.

The festival has begun. Loud fireworks crackle and snap against the sky. Laughter fills the air, music and the sound of feet tapping.

"Can we try it now?" Tiller asks, turning away from the dances starting up.

For my part, I watch with an odd sense of hollowness. Those are the matching dances. The pairing two-step. The Third-Hand hop. The twisted tangle. Everyone who isn't matched dances, and by the end of the night market most everyone will have found their heart mates. Tiller and I have never danced, though. Because secretly, I know neither of us wants to.

More secretly, because I want the rules to change and for the world to tell me what I already know: that my heart mate is sitting in this air contraption with me. About to be airborne.

The first song ends, and a low horn takes over instead, marking the opening of the market shops. Overhead, the Sun Temple's bells ring through the air, loud and crystal clear. The merchants lift the wood-framed roofs of their carts while others tie open the flaps of fiber-cloth tents. Each booth has its own symbols, its own familial patterns carved into beams or painted onto fiber posters or flying from hand-stitched flags and twist-tie dyed banners.

Small strings of flags in all colors of the rainbow stream between the ancient beams of the Sun Temple. Each flag bears an emblem and a name. Every lineage of every family in town has a line of flags in matching hues. Mine and Tillers' family line has always hung at opposite ends from one another-the flaming red cooks being Tiller's history and the green viney healers being mine.

All strings, regardless of origin point, meet in the middle of the roof of the highest silver and crystal dome of the Sun Temple. The last place the day's light touches.

This magnificent gem-studded, silver filigree and crystal windowed turret is the most historical place in all the town. It marks the very spot where the first child-birthing pair gave birth to the first set of triplets. These triplets: named Carry (he), Weigh (she), and Hand (ze) would grow and establish the complex dance of mating and birthing rituals of our town.

A birthing pair, Receiver and Giver, is never to be matched without a neutral Third-Hand to support the family. So history tells us, so the codes of life go. All the families are very strict on this. No match is ever to be cut short. No person is ever to be left isolated and alone.

Which for Tiller and me, spells doom. Because, despite our closeness-Tiller and I both know we will never live together. Never support a family together. Never grow old under the same banner of flags. Never ever rest beside one another in the same grass bed.

Whether we both long for it, or not.

Bending to tradition is what has kept our town alive through all the weather the world has thrown at us. Who would we be to break such strong ropes?

"You okay?" Tiller asks me, zer soft hand on my forearm.

I shiver, not from the chill of oncoming night, but from the warmth of Tiller's touch.

Desire flares up like a fire in my heart, hot and spreading fast through my whole body, down to my toes and fingertips. I look up at the streamers, and the feeling curls up to die inside the bottom of my lungs like a long, aching sigh I can never breathe out.

"I'm fine," I say because I have to be.

"Well, you two coming?" Tan asks, sitting on the back of the cruise, legs wrapped around the tail, waiting for us to get going.

"You're flying with us?" I balk. "Is that safe?"

Tan nods, grinning big. "Do it all the time with my family."

Tiller and I glance at each other, shrug, and both stall, a little scared of flying for the first time.

"Don't worry. It's easier than it looks," Tan encourages us without prompting.

Both Tiller and I take a breath in, sucking slow and steady. Getting ready. I push my three sky gems into the slot designed for them. The contraption hisses and grumbles like its waking up for the first time. I look over my controls and remember Tan's words:

Push and pull the rudder to stay on course. Use the wheel to adjust the sails. Keep plenty of air in the sails at all times and aim the nose of the cruiser wherever we want to go. The gems provide the lift and thrust, ie. all the hard complicated parts.

Tan gives the ground a little kick to get us moving, Tiller aims the rudder straight on, I crank the wheel to tighten the sail, and then-we're flying!

"It's surprisingly relaxing," both Tiller and I shout into the wind.

Behind us, Tan's laughter is intoxicating.

And suddenly I feel this funny feeling. Like the three of us are a family. Like we've just been out there on the floor dancing and the stones in our necklaces all lit up. We've been matched, and this is our celebratory flight. And tonight, we'll drink the sweet water of the white whipper flowers' seed-the tincture of love. We'll all fall asleep, and when we wake, we'll feel fuller than ever with our lives bonded for life.

Only, this silly wish makes no sense. Tiller and I are both Thirds and Tan is a Giver who looks half like a Receiver and maybe can't actually do either with her conflicted body. And yet, that's exactly why it all feels so right. We're all different, which makes us, somehow, a good fit.

"Hold on!" Tiller says from behind. "Something's wrong."

I come to and see we've been swallowed by an ominous dark matte of clouds. I try to spin the wheel and swing us out of the cloud, but to no avail. I can hear Tiller working the rudder, back and forth, back and forth. Only, we aren't going anywhere at all.

"Snap out of it, Shadow!" Tiller barks at me, except this time the voice is closer, more present.

I blink, coming to, and see that we've flown into nothing but an ordinary cloud. The air is a little damp and chilly, but nothing to worry about. I easily swing us out.

"Sorry about that," I say, abashed.

"Noob," Tan ribs me.

Together, we laugh. The sound echoes around the cloud, and with each reverberation I feel lighter. And we all three sound happier than before. My chest tightens around the joy brimming inside of me. If only this could last. This moment, flying through the air, with Tiller whom I deeply love and Tan who fits us so well.

Wait…what? Love? I can't allow myself to think these thoughts.

"You know what I was thinking?" Tan's voice cuts in, as if responding to my thoughts. "We could ditch the festival this star-cycle. Fly up to the top of the Sun Tower instead. I hear the view from up there is unlike you can see anywhere else in all the world."

"Sounds good," Tiller and I say in unison without a breath's hesitation.

Anything is better than having to dance the courting dance when all you feel like doing is being with the people you know you can't stay with.

Again, I see White Fur's stoic, unsmiling face as I've imagined it in my mind.

Not that I would know what White Fur's face looks like. I've only ever heard my birthing pair talk about zer, and only ever in vague terms. So I know the image I've dreamed up is a projection of my own ideas surrounding zer. And yet, over the course of my growing adulthood, that image has become strangely more important. Like my heart knows something I don't.

Tiller aims us for the roof of the Sun Temple. Up there, there's a round courtyard where Tan instructs us how to bring the air cruiser down soft. It swooshes through the grass with a gentle bumping and rocking. We laugh together as the cruiser slows to a stop. Getting up, Tan points at a small copper gate that leads into the Temple's inner garden where vines form tall tower-like walls. On the other side, a flagstone path leads to a stairwell that's lit by small star-shaped lanterns. The garden smells floral and bursting with life.

Tan holds the gate open for us and we move through all together into the inner sanctuary. Red and purple flowers bloom everywhere. Blades of emerald black striped grass bend in a sudden sharp breeze, shaking as if they're cold.

I'm reminded of the tremor Tiller and I felt in the field. My heart starts to pound. What if it really was just a precursor to something horrible?

"Check this out," Tan says several steps ahead of both Tiller and me.

Tan opens a stone door against the garden's far wall. The door's surface is polished and smooth. There's not a single decoration. No gems studded into complex carvings like the rest of the Sun Temple. No crystal figurines holding up tiny suns. No glowing star-stones that stay warm all night with the sun's energy. No gem-speckled drawings depicting the history of our people and the world. Just a grey flat stone door. It looks impressively unimpressive. Something I'd have ignored had I come up this way alone.

"In here," Tan calls from inside.

Tiller goes in first, and I follow, nervous. Inside, I can barely make out the trace outline of Tan waving us on. I rush down several steps without stopping, just in case I freeze up. What's there to be so scared of? This is just some storage room on the roof of the Sun Temple. A place where the festival banners and flag streamers go after the night market closes up. The place where the bells are stored for repairs.

Nothing to worry about.

The steps lead down to another door, this one already hanging open. Inside, I can see there's light again. It's warm and soft, a dull yellow glow like the stone is glowing. I step into the room and look to Tiller for reassurance. Tiller gives me an all's-good circle with zer index finger and thumb. I relax and breathe in the musty air. It smells like no one has been in here in a long while.

Storage room, sure. An unused storage room at the bottom of a bunch of weirdly dark and featureless stone stairs. A storage room that glows from its own walls. Yep, that's not at all weird.

"Well? What do you think?" Tan asks from the middle of the room.

"What is this place?" Tiller asks before I can.

"The room of the Third-Hand Prophecy," Tan says, which explains nothing.

I sputter from the blow of those words. What could Tan possibly mean? What prophecy? I glance sidelong across my shoulder to see Tiller's posture. Ze is standing with arms at zer sides, head tucked. Like ze isn't shocked. No, worse. Like ze knows something I don't. I ignore that feeling and turn back to Tan.

"I'm sorry, what did you say?" I ask, wondering if I heard wrong.

"The Third-Hand Prophecy," Tan repeats and clicks her tongue.

I look around the room. There is a wall, all black, with a map of the world painted on it. There are symbols for each of the four directions. A single human stands at the point of each direction, reaching hands forward. In the center is a kind of swirling windstorm. I feel a flicker of something from a vision. Something about four people saving the world.

A flash of darkness bites at my mind, sweeping the bright thought away.

I blink and stare at the painting, suddenly afraid, and I don't know why.

"I don't get what any of this is," I say, confused.

"I figured, what with you being in love with Tiller, you'd have seen it. But then, maybe Weavebreak and Moonshade never explained like they should have…" Tan fades off, scratching her furrowed forehead in confusion.

"I'm sorry, did you say Weavebreak and Moonshade?" I balk.

My birthing pair? Why?

"Well, of course I did."

"What do you know about this?" I remember how different she is from the usual Giver. "Are you…involved in this prophesy?"

"No, silly. I'm just a regular old towns person. Unlike you two. The prophecy is connected to the familial line of White Fur and those they love."

"White Fur?" I gasp.

"Well, of course. The other double-Third. I mean, I suppose the spirit could have attached itself to Nimbus' lineage, but then we'd never have known what was coming. And clearly you do, so…"

"Know what?" I ask, arms hugging tight around my middle, tense and scared. What was this about Nimbus, too? I take a few strides, right up into Tan's face. We stand nose to throat, not nose to nose like Tiller and I. Tan is a Giver, and so she stands a whole two hands taller than me. I glare up into her face with as sharp of a look as I can manage. Brow tight, jaw stiff, lips pursed. "What does any of this have to do with me? I don't have any special skills."

"Sure you do."

To my surprise, it's Tiller who's talking, not Tan.

I turn on Tiller, mouth gaping like a doorway. "What?"

"Your visions, sensing that earthquake," Tiller explains.

But those words are no explanation, and I'm more confused by them than ever. "What do you mean? You felt it too!"

"Because I was touching you," Tiller says with a blush.

And suddenly, I get a combination of complicated feelings-none of which I like. The first is that Tiller and Tan, and Weavebreak and Moonshade (apparently), knew that I was different. That I have some kind of something special. Some…talent. That I see and feel and think things other people don't. Which ties in directly to my second, more awful thought-that a badness is really coming, if they all believe in my talent.

But then, instead of care about that, I think a final, more awful thought. That this ability to see into a grim future, this talent to save others, is what Tiller has been fascinated about in me. What if Tiller did not want me, Shadowscape, the lost Third-Hand who's just about to be forced into full adulthood by mating with those not of his choosing-who was really, actually in love with someone ze knows ze can never have.

I sigh, heavy and loud. Because, I realize, I have been hoping for more. Not just the love that Third-Hands usually show each other, a kind companionship in kind. But a special love. Something for just Tiller and me. Something big and meaningful.

My shoulders collapse in defeat. My arms flop useless by my side and my chest caves in. My knees bend without me telling them to, and before I know it I'm sitting on the biting stone of this unusually chilly room. Except even that perception is wrong. We're supposed to be in the Sun Temple. Things are supposed to be sunny. Warm to the touch. Reassuring. But instead, I'm sitting in a pool of my own darkness surrounded by nothing but the touch of ice.

"Hey! Snap out of it!" Tiller is shouting.

I glance up, but everyone looks farther away than they were a second ago. Like they've all decided to walk away and leave me here alone. Wouldn't be the first time. I think I see White Fur's face again, and suddenly the cold all around me makes sense. It's the cold of fear. The cold of abandonment. Of feeling just like I feel right now. Without love.

"Shadow, come on. Snap out of it," Tan joins Tiller in calling to me.

But they're too late. Aren't they?

The ground starts to shake. Not a little tremor this time, but big fat waves that curl the stone underneath me and crack it along the seams like a bit of inflexible rock candy. I feel the vibrations channeling through my body, up through my bones, and coming out of my extremities like static electricity jumping from my fingertips. The temperature in the room drops even lower than before and I start to shiver. My teeth chatter, filling the room with a clacking-clicking noise that only adds to the low rumble in a way that sounds like nightmare music.

Sounds I remember from my dreams.

What came next in my dreams? The Sun Temple falls, the town is covered in a massive dark cloud, and everybody dies.

No. This can't be happening. I force myself to my feet, shuddering and unsteady as I am. I try to take a step and fall back down. My knees hit the stone with a dual crack, and it's so cold down here that I don't think I'll ever get up again, let alone run out of here and save my town. So much for "special talents." Turns out everyone was wrong about me. I can't do anything right. Can't even save Tiller and Tan who are standing in the same awful room.

"No! Shadow!" I hear in a foggy, hazy way. A hundred worlds away.

But then a stab of warmth penetrates the cold. Like a bright ray of glowing hot sunlight on a winter's day, the heat rushes right through me. I gasp from the shock of how all-over warm it is. I feel every cell wake back up, my skin come back to life, my bones thaw. It presses against my chest and wraps my whole body up like the biggest, thickest blanket I've ever felt. Even my eyeballs feel like they've been cracked free from ice, and I can move them again.

I blink, cold tears stinging my eyes, and when the blur clears I see the bright orange tangle of Tiller's hair pressed against my shoulder. Zer arms tight around my whole body. Zer hair, zer wood gold skin, zer brilliant purple eyes-everything is lit up with emotion for me. Glowing like bright star light. And I can see where zer skin touches mine, I'm glowing just as bright.

Zer breath, like a new harvest breeze, warm and damp, sweeps across my earlobe. "You're trancing. You need to come out of it so we can help people. Please, come back to me."

My heart hammers against my ribs as Tiller's words repeat in my mind. "Come back to me."

Tiller wants me? Even when I'm spouting scary visions?

I feel the warmth inside of me say yes as it curls fingers around my body, drawing me away from the cold, away from the shadow, away from the dark of no hope.

I feel my body melt against Tiller's frame. Only, I can feel both of our bodies collapsing because neither of us is strong enough to support the weight of us together. Then, a third arm, neither hot nor cold comes to support us both. Tan lifts us back to our feet, rights us so we can lean on one another and find footing.

I think for a second, brief and passing, that I now understand how families are supposed to work. The hot fire of the Giver and the cool water of the Receiver and the neutral balance of the Third-Hand. Only here, we three don't match the rules, the way the elders have told us love has to be.

Yet, our love sings the same.

"Come on, you two. We have to get out of here," Tan-our third hand, in a way-calls above the din of the rumbling stone.

I realize the temple collapsing had not happened yet; my vision had been a warning. We rush up the breaking, moving stairs and come out the door onto the roof. All around us, the Sun Temple is coming undone. The tall, once glorious towers to our left and right crash to the ground. Screams of our townspeople pierce the air from far below. And I hope-oh, I hope-they can get to safety. I hope they've prepared for the worst after our warning earlier that night.

The emergency horn slices through the air, high pitched and warbling, and I know that at least some people have heeded our warning.

"We have to use the air cruiser to get out of here," Tan says from up ahead.

The three of us don't say another word but rush to the ship. Tan takes over the driver's wheel, whips us into the air, circles the Temple once, and brings us in for landing on the stilled ground close to the town buildings, safe and sound. Once we touch down, we stumble off the cruiser, trying to take stock of the mess around us.

Only a huge dark cloud has descended, blotting out the stars and lights of the town.

"We have to see if anyone else is alive," Tan says.

We all agree silently and start scrambling across rubble piles until our feet are on flat ground. Not flat as it once was, all groomed and tidy. But flat in the sense that there's no chunks of stone to clamber over.

We find the faint silhouette of bodies, the surviving townspeople huddled together. Tan motions for Tiller and me to wait where we are, then rushes over and talks in a hushed tone. I can hear the edges of Tan's questions: asking if people are missing, if they

have water, is anyone hurt, and so on. The people are mostly silent, shocked and scared, heads bowed. The silence of those suddenly plunged into disaster.

"At least we warned them," Tiller tries to cheer me up.

It doesn't work. Because, somehow, some piece of me knew this would befall us long ago. I knew and stayed silent; I doubted my own abilities. Because if I did not truly believe, if I stayed silent, it was as if that saved loved ones, families, homes. My nightmare visions only amount to guilt, now. The guilt of knowing the truth before knowing what it means.

It was the end of the town. The falling of the Sun Temple. A curse of darkness, descending on us all.

"Hindsight can be the enemy of wisdom," says a voice I know well.

"Weavebreak," I say and my voice catches.

"We knew you had the visions," comes the paired voice that is always close behind Weavebreak's. "We knew and always loved you."

"Moonshade!" I exclaim, turning to reach for their two pairs of arms. "Thank the stars and sun. You're both safe."

Only I turn around and touch no one. Nothing. I narrow my eyes, trying to see through the darkness that's like the height of midnight, but I see nothing. They can't be that far away from me; I heard their voices like they were just right beside me. On my right or left. I step out into the darkness, searching for footing, reaching my hands wide. Only, both my hands come back empty, full of cold air. I frown, confused, about to ask where they are hiding when it hits me.

They aren't hiding.

They're dead.

These voices aren't their true voices, but ghosts inside my bones and cells. The remnant of their energies stored up inside me, the soft imprint of their genes upon mine, reaching out to me through our familial bond to talk to me one last time through my ability to see what is not there.

My eyes burn with a hotness that tightens my chest and seals my mouth shut in a thick, downward line. Streams weave their way down my burning cheeks and meet in a single droplet at my chin. I dash it away with the back of my wrist.

It takes all my strength to not fall to the ground and curl up into a baby's tight ball and try to sleep these nightmares away. I can't have lost my whole family. I can't.

Then, a hand touches my elbow. It's gentle yet firm.

"What's wrong?" Tiller asks innocently.

"My family…" I choke. "They're…I had…am having a vision…and…"

I can't say the words out loud. I just can't. My throat closes up and silent tears stream down my cheeks.

"I'm so sorry, Shadow," Tiller says and zer voice cracks too.

Like my heart.

I sob, grabbing Tiller like ze is the only rock, the only steady ground, the last stronghold left. Tan, steady and strong, returns to my side and stands close, supporting me like a structure I know can trust. I let my head fall onto Tan's shoulder while Tiller wraps arms around my middle, holding me up so I don't fall.

My knees turn to jelly, but I'm buoyed by my pair. My pair…

I shouldn't think it, but I am so glad these are the two here. My double-Third and my Giver who is also part Receiver.

"We're so sorry we didn't tell you, Shadowscape," says Weavebreak's voice inside my veins, and I feel Tan jump slightly in surprise and Tiller's grip tighten around my waist, their connection with me allowing them to also hear Weavebreak's words, our forming bond tying them into my vision.

"Tell me? Tell me what?" I say out loud into Tiller's shoulder.

"That we knew." The voice did not belong to my birth-makers' ghosts. But a living voice.

Tan.

I jerk up, stunned, my face a tight glare. I know Tan can't see my expression for all this darkness, but I glare all the same. It makes me feel a modicum better having someone living to be angry with. Tan, a conduit to how awful I feel.

"You?" I bite. "You knew this was coming?"

"Not exactly," Tiller adds.

"We knew you've been having important visions, is what I mean. I went to talk to Weavebreak and Moonshade about it a moon ago. We figured it had to be more than just dreams," Tan explains.

"As your visions increased-it seemed clear White Fur was reaching for you-we began to realize the great darkness was coming," Weavebreak adds, vibrating my insides with the old hum of her strong, booming voice.

"And that you-like White Fur-would need to leave town one day soon," Moonshade added, voice breaking.

"Only, we never thought like this," Weavebreak says, and the words are so quiet I barely feel them vibrating the ribs in my chest. Like a sigh I've been holding in, have been meaning for star-cycles to let out.

That's Weavebreak's breath inside me, I realize. Her dread of this day come.

I sag, collapsing on Tiller's arm, all my rage snuffed out.

"We all have a lot to explain," Tiller says, close to my ear.

I reel back away from Tiller, my eyes narrow and flashing with what? Fear? Hurt? Confusion? Resignation? All of the above. In my haste, I crash into something behind me, smacking my back and rattling my brain. When I put my hand against my cheek, tears wet my palm.

"You too?" I say in a mere whisper.

Tiller says nothing which is as good as a yes.

"Did the whole town know?" I ask.

"Yes," Moonshade says, his voice a breathless gasp that matches mine. "But only in theory. We guessed you had the same power White Fur had, but we had no way to verify until it came to pass."

"You could have asked," I think but don't say.

I don't even know if that's true. If anyone had asked me about my visions-even Tiller-

would I have confessed? No, probably not. Because I had still been pretending, acting like those dark dreams didn't matter. Because I didn't want them to. I didn't want a great dark cloud to come over my town. I didn't want the Sun Temple to fall. I didn't want to lose everyone I love. And I didn't want to run away my home like White Fur had, leaving a wake of sadness behind me.

"I'm going with you, though," Tiller says as if I've said all this aloud.

With Tiller, I don't have to. At least that much is still true.

"Where will we go?" I ask, not sure who I'm asking.

"To find White Fur in the Northern Kingdom," Tan says.

I blink. "The Northern Kingdom?"

"Indeed," Weavebreak confirms. "That's where ze left with zer lover, Nimbus."

"Zer what?!" I balk, but then instantly the shock is gone.

Of course, White Fur had a lover who wasn't Weavebreak and Moonshade. Of course, White Fur left us for love. Why hadn't I ever thought of that? I understood, for inside my own heart, the desire burned just as bright. I touch Tiller's arm, who hasn't let me go this whole time, and I know. It all makes so much sense now.

"Nimbus was a Third-Hand, weren't ze?" I ask because I see now what's happening.

"Indeed," Weavebreak says and her voice falls.

I am struck with a memory. Weavebreak standing out in a field. A breeze blows and sunlight catches the small braid that she always kept at her temple with a single white feather woven into it. A reminder, she used to say, of someone great. White Fur, of course. In my imagination, this braid falls in front of her beautiful sky-blue eyes. And a hand, pale as morning sunlight speckled with flecks of gold, brushes it away. Weavebreak giggles and her mouth forms the shape of a name: White Fur. And in saying that name, she sounds more at peace than she ever did in my life. As if she knows the whole world is safe.

"White Fur met Nimbus in a vision," Weavebreak goes on. "A Third-Hand from another tribe-the Andui in the north. Nimbus came to us after having a vision of White Fur and their joint potential power. You have, of course, inherited that same power through White Fur's careful tending while you were just a babe. When Moonshade and I no longer needed White Fur's aide, we gave zer our blessing to go live among the Andui. And now, you and Tiller must go join them in the North. There you will learn where you belong.

"And," Weavebreak adds, "you will learn how to save the world using what you learn."

The heart goes where it wants.

It was never just about feelings, that proverb. It was about actually leaving. About loving the world and your people so much that you'd go anywhere and do anything for them. And about loving someone so much you'd go with them to the northernmost ends of the world to find a place where you would be accepted. To the Northern Kingdom. To the Andui.

"Weavebreak confirmed. Nimbus is in the North," I say.

Tiller takes my hand in zers. "Then, let's go. Only, how?"

"The air cruiser," Tan says. "My family has been building it for generations, waiting for the moment it was needed. And packed inside, you have all the supplies you need to make it to the next town. I made a deal with Tiller's family before festival. Loads of travel sacks full of preserves, road ready. Just in case."

"My family knew?" Tiller asks, as shocked as I've been this whole time.

And in that, I can't help but feel a little bit better. Less alone.

"I may have mentioned you might leave town on an important mission with Shadow," Tan says, sounding a mixture of proud and ashamed.

"Thank you," Tiller whispers. "I wouldn't want them to worry about me, thinking I ran off or died in the shake."

I think of White Fur. Then, I think of my own family-lost, even as they continue to talk in my mind. My heart breaks just like it did in my vision of the dark. The ice-cold daggers of loneliness stab through my chest.

But then, I feel Tiller's hand in mine, and that makes the refocus easier than it would have been alone.

I breathe in slow, holding back my sobs, focusing instead on the people who've survived. On the shapes we saw huddled together. And, I focus on action, on the mission. On the vision-version of Weavebreak and Moonshade. Of White Fur calling to me. I tighten the strap on my belly pouch, sucking in my gut. "I'm ready," I say.

"How will we know which way to go?" Tiller asks in a hush.

"Follow your heart," Weavebreak says inside of me and I know Tan and Tiller can no longer hear her. She is fading, moving on with Moonshade.

"The visions will still come to me, won't they?" I ask aloud, wanting her to stay.

"Who are you asking?" Tiller asks.

"My family," I explain, coloring. It's weird to acknowledge you have skills other people don't. But then, I guess I've always been different. Lack of focus, others called it. Or attention deficit.

Unique, Tiller always said. Like I had something special instead of something wrong with me.

"I can no longer hear them. Your family," Tiller adds, zer eyes sad.

"Yes. They are now a part of me. Like the visions. There but not there."

"We're bound to you by love," Moonshade says. "Like White Fur and Nimbus."

I repeat the words aloud for Tiller and Tan to hear. And in saying them, I know they are true. The visions are connected to love. Love for the land. Love for the world. Love for our people. Love of family and friend. That's why I saw this dark coming. White Fur was trying to tell me something.

"It's going to be okay. We're going to find White Fur, and we're going to fix the world," I say, and my voice sounds deeper, stronger, older than it ever has.

It sounds like what I think White Fur would sound like.

As if in confirmation, I see in my mind's eye a string of flags, waving at me in a breeze. Two lines, connecting. On one, my line with Weavebreak and Moonshade. And on another, a glowing line with flags-all bright white.

"That line," a voice says, "represents the way to the Andui."

I know now, beyond a shadow of a doubt, that voice inside of me is White Fur, ready to guide us north.

"Let's go," I say aloud to Tiller, reluctantly pulling away from Tan's pillar of support, wishing there was some way she could come with us, too.

"Okay," Tiller says, and I feel zer fingers curl around my knuckles. And, despite all the sorrow still pooling in my chest, I feel that hope. The warm security of love.

"Wait," Tiller says before we leave the rubble. Ze let go of my hand, and I hear a rustling at the ground. A shifting of stones. A rattling of pebbles and a slight tremble of the earth.

"Got it," Tiller says and rights zerself.

"A rock?" I ask.

"Not just any rock, it's an eye geode," Tiller says and puts it in my palm. "A memento of home."

I take it and roll it between my fingers, feeling all of its uneven edges. It feels like my heart right now. Jagged and complicated. There's still something beautiful about it, though. About life.

"Thank you," I say, my voice catching.

"Can I give you something else?" Tiller asks.

I blush, feeling my whole body turn warm. I know exactly what Tiller is thinking. And I'm thinking it to. Just like my fingers against the sharp edges of this geode, I want to feel Tiller's hands against the sharp edges of me.

"Yes. Yes, of course," I say, cheeks hot, lips dry.

I lick them because I'm scared. I've never kissed anyone before.

Tiller leans in, and I can feel the ecstatic energy of our blending. The sheer force of two hearts facing the same direction, aimed at the same goal. And for the first time in all of our friendship, I know beyond a shadow of a doubt that this-right here-this is love.

And love, I finally understand, is the biggest and deepest kind of magic. It exists both within and outside of the small limits of our one single town. It is the endless lifeblood of the universe. And with it, Tiller and I really can reach the North. We can find White Fur, and together with Nimbus-the four of us can change the very shape of reality. Like those four small people in the painting back at the Sun Temple. The waves of our actions will ripple across the whole world, and the effects will echo in the cells and bones of reality for all time.

This is the power of the double-Thirds. The power to grow love, bringing it to bloom like new flowers all across the world. And, if we trust in love, it's glowing light will lessen the dark because love doesn't just give hope, it multiplies it. We can have visions that help save the people from calamity, but also show that love in all form heals.

Tiller pulls away from me, our lips separating slowly, yet I can still feel the vibration of heat and passion humming between us. I signal a new secret hand gesture: one finger against my lips. And in this, I know Tiller will understand I'm saying: forever yours.

I feel Tiller gesture back in the darkness, and the warmth in my heart spreads to my extremities, down through the bottoms of my feet and the palms of my hands, radiating out into the air around me. At the horizon, the sun comes up and a bar of light strikes Tiller and me.

"I love you," Tiller says out loud, reaching for my hand.

"I love you, too," I say, reaching back.

Our palms meet.

"Now, let's go save the world," we say in unison, like we always do.

I pause, glancing back over my shoulder. In the new day's light, I see the ruins of the town. Of both our homes. A single streamer flies between them, clinging onto a tile of my roof and attaching itself, flapping, to the cornerstone of Tiller's. I can't help but think our elongated shadows look like arms, reaching out.

Then, I see Tan crouched beside a line of people waiting for bandages.

"Come with us," I say suddenly.

Tan looks up, sad. "I can't."

"Why not?" Tiller asks from beside me.

My heart gives a jump. I wasn't alone in feeling it when we were flying. That sensation that the three of us belonged together. That we were a matched set. That this was a family and we needed one another.

And yet, did Tan not feel it the same as Tiller and me? Were we both equally wrong in that?

"I'm needed here," Tan says, voice low and dark.

Oh. Of course, it makes sense. I have my heart to follow. My visions to go off of. And Tiller had always been alongside me. The double to my Third. But where did that leave Tan?

Here. To rebuild.

"I understand," Tiller says before I can get the words out.

"So do I," I say, my hands pressed together, bent in a low bow. "You need to stay."

"Thank you," Tan says, then hesitates as if there's more to say.

"No, thank you. For everything," I'm about to say, but my throat catches and another tear rolls down my cheek. We are forever parting ways. Our hearts aren't going where they want, but where they are needed most. Tiller and I, to the north. And Tan, here among the people we leave behind.

Just like Weavebreak and Moonshade stayed for me when White Fur left for the North.

Only, wait. Since it appears what we three are experiencing is love, then-I remembered what Moonshade said:

"I'll see you in visions," I say to Tan. "And I'll tell you things about us."

"Like letters in your dreams," Tiller adds.

I hear Tan's voice catch. "I wish I could send back."

I reach out and put my hand on Tan's shoulder, pulling her into a hug. "Who knows, maybe one day you can."

"We can hope," Tan says, close to my ear.

She's like a perfect Third-hand, I can't help but thinking. Supporting both Tiller and I in what we have to do alone. Giving us the strength we need to carry on.

A soft breeze kicks up and brushes my cheek, and it feels like my birthing pairs' hands reassuring me after a nightmare. Reminding me that White Fur loved me even if ze were gone. The air grabs the wayward tendrils of my hair, sweeping past my ears and the sounds are like the singing and dancing of our people at the height of their pleasure. I can smell the caramel and fresh baked bread wafting in the air, sweet and wheat-filled. I can see the Sun Temple, catching light and glowing in the last moments of day. The soft memory is a boon that lightens my step. I nod, more to myself than to anyone. Then, I turn full body away from the old, and face a whole new open road.

I breathe in and start to move with Tiller, and sure enough, my heart knows just where to go.

Our next step is perfectly in line with one another, stride for stride. Just as we've always done. I tighten my grip on Tiller's hand and feel the same tension given back. I breathe in, lungs full of air.

We're ready, hearts open wide. We can face whatever may come our way.

And no matter what, the three of us have love. Our forever bond.

And that's going to be enough to save the world.

Find Gracie Wilson in the trees enjoying nature's wonders, traveling to see the latest animal conservations, or at aquariums all around the world. This girl loves nature and all animals. She has many pets and is always adding new additions. The more the merrier in her mind. Sitting under the shade reading a book, letting the world around her pass by, while she is safe in her bubble of imagination. Well that is where she'd love to stay. She is a #1 Amazon Bestselling Author from Ontario, Canada. She is a first generation Canadian living in Ontario. Her family is from Scotland, so finding her in the hot sun for very long is unlikely, but give her rain and thunderstorms and she's golden.

BEAUTIFULLY IMAGINED

The Beautifully Series

by Gracie Wilson

"Imagine if those defining moments in life never came to be due to the fear of the unknown. Playing it safe, never risking more than you're willing to lose. Life can be beautiful and everything you imagined, if only you take that leap."

—Gracie Wilson

CHAPTER ONE

Imagine I said yes…

Standing outside my dorm room, waiting, I can feel the shiver of fear but the tingling of anticipation too. When Reed called me out of the blue asking if I needed a ride to Galveston, Texas, for his dad's 50th party cruise I was shocked. Not because he and I don't talk, but because we don't attend the same University. I'm a first year at the University of Texas in Austin, and he is in his final year in Houston. I'm completely out of the way and he would have to backtrack a couple hours to get me. He doesn't seem to care though. I told him I'd be fine to drive myself and when he wasn't okay with that almost four-hour drive alone, I tried saying I could take the bus to him, at least. That didn't fly either. So now he is on his way here. Instead of the

hour drive for him it would have taken, it will now be a seven hour round trip for him.

Reed and I have known each other since I was six, when I moved to Michigan with my family. Starting at a new school with an Alabama accent was something that people loved to tease me about. The older I got, the less distinguished my accent was; I now sound like the rest of them.

His sister Danni and I became fast friends, which meant he tormented me every chance he got for a long time. He was three years older than us, but he still had gone out of his way to trip me and throw snowballs at me. Which was something I wasn't prepared for, being from Alabama.

When I got to high school, I had hoped he'd finally open his eyes and see me. But I was a freshman and he was a senior, so apparently that meant that we were from different worlds. It seemed like we'd *always* be from different worlds. The only saving grace was his cousin Derek. When Reed was ignoring me, Derek would talk to me, help me when there were problems at school.

Derek and Reed are the same age so I never understood why he could act as though he could see me, but Reed couldn't. *Wouldn't* was more like it. When we were in the school halls, I was no one—he looked right over me—but at home it seemed he'd always go out of his way to run into me.

It all changed, or so I thought, the week before he left for the University of Houston. There were mistaken touches that I knew weren't by accident, moments I knew he was going to say something. Then the night before he left we'd all been at a party. The only reason I was there was because I'd been invited by Derek. When I got there, Reed was shocked, to say the least. His eyes kept drifting back to me, even when he was talking to someone else. The girl he had gone with had taken a back seat and he was no longer showing her interest. He spent the whole night next to me and would only leave me with Derek, if he had to move further away. It was odd, but nothing prepared me for the moment he walked me home.

"You'll be careful, won't you?" Reed asked. His voice startled me. What was he talking about? "I mean Derek and I won't be here to look out for you anymore."

I was taken aback by his words. Part of me wanted to be belligerent and tell him that he has no say, since he ignores me, but I didn't want to ruin his mood or the fact that it was just him and I, together.

"I can look after myself. Don't worry, I'll make sure Danni is okay too. You go off and become that big time accountant you want to be and I will just be little old me." I said, but there was sadness in my voice.

"Dad wants me to be an accountant. I'm not sure if it's for me."

Reed never talked like this. He'd always had a plan: he was going to be an accountant, work with his dad and take over the firm.

"Oh." I said quietly.

"Can I tell you something? You can't tell anyone. Not even Danni."

His words made my heart race. He was confiding in me, which wasn't something he's ever done before. He's told me some things, but never told me not to tell Danni. "I won't say anything if you don't want me to. I wouldn't do that to you, Reed." I said softly and he took a step towards me, placing his hand on the side of my face.

"Someday, someone is going to come in and try to take away all the sweetness that you have here. You need to protect yourself because I never want you to lose this side of you." His words floored me. He'd never spoken to me this way before and I can't imagine never hearing him talk to me this way again. He took his hand away slowly and I felt heat rise to my cheeks. "Promise me you will protect yourself, always. No matter who you are with."

I didn't know what to do so I nodded. "I promise."

"When I start school, I'm not starting as an accountant. I'm majoring in Anthropology with a minor in Law, Values, and Policy Minor." My mouth dropped open. I knew what this meant. His dad was going to flip his shit when he found out. "I haven't told them yet. I will—I won't ask you to lie about it. No one has to know you knew before the rest of them, but I had to tell someone."

"Why me?" I asked daringly.

He leaned in and I was still unsure what to do. His lips pressed against mine causing my body to come to life. My hands found their way to his chest and I pulled him closer by the shirt, slowly deepening our contact. His hands gripped my hips tightly pulling me so close that there wasn't any space between us. I felt free. When he pulled away, I felt the world come crawling back around us. "That's why."

When I woke up the next morning there was a letter waiting for me. It was from Reed and it broke

my heart. I thought we'd started something special enough to warrant a personal goodbye.

I couldn't do it—say goodbye in person. I'm sorry. I'll see you over the holidays. Leaving you behind is one of the hardest things I've ever done. Protect yourself.

R.

He never came home for the holidays. Instead he invited the family to visit him in Texas. Without me, of course, and I never heard from him until he came home that summer. By then, everything he warned me about had come true. He had moved on. I must not have meant anything to him, because it was so easy for him to move on from me. Whereas I had played that night over and over again in my head, he had decided it never happened.

Derek didn't understand what had happened to us as a group. When Reed continued to make up reasons to keep away from me, Derek started to get annoyed and questioned it all. It only made things worse. Reed would just get pissed and storm off. Derek and Reed even got into a physical fight once. I wasn't sure why until I heard Derek tell him that maybe he wouldn't have been too attentive to me if Reed would get his head out of his ass and stop acting like I didn't exist. After that fight Reed didn't make excuses to leave but he did start referring to me as 'Kid' instead of anything else. That hurt.

The next two summers continued in this same pattern, which was why this summer, before I started University, I left. No way was I going to wait around for another summer of him ignoring me. He never got close to me; it was like he was allergic to my skin, always making sure we had no contact. I got the hint. He didn't need to continue pouring salt on the wounds.

I was friend zoned, if I could even call it that—I wasn't even sure if we were even friends anymore. So I went to spend the summer in Alabama with my cousins before starting at University of Texas in Austin. I had gotten accepted into Houston, too, but I couldn't go there. Not with how things had been between us those other summers. I accepted Austin for what it was: as close to Reed as I'd ever get again.

Something changed suddenly though. He started texting me this last summer and emailing me when school started up. It felt like before that night, back before he left for University. It was nice, but I would do what he had told me to do that night. Protect myself, even if it was against him. I could no longer trust my heart.

Unexpectedly, I hear the honking of his truck and look up to see him pulling up in front of me. He gets out of his truck and comes around, quickly wrapping his arms around me, squeezing me tightly.

I'm too shocked to stick to my resolve. *Reed is actually hugging me!* He lets go and grabs my bag from my hand. Going over to the bed of his truck, he puts my bag beside his.

Hopping in the truck with him, I just stare. I can't believe I said yes to the ride and am now sitting here with him.

"Hey, Kid," Reed says and his smile can light up the world. He has blond hair and crystal blue eyes that look like clear oceans.

"I'm *not* a kid," I say rudely as the flashbacks of him the past few summers come tumbling back. Maybe things haven't changed like I had thought. I'm still just a kid to him. I'm sure all he sees in me is that red-headed little girl with freckles. I'm a classic ginger with pale skin and baby blue eyes. Nothing extraordinary about me, not like him. He's perfect, which is why I know I'm way out of my league here.

Looking back at me, he has an odd smirk on his face that I just can't get a read on. He shakes his head and puts the truck into drive. "Well, this is going to be a fun."

CHAPTER TWO

Imagine I got in the truck…

Ever wish you could be anywhere else? Well, that's exactly what I'm feeling right now. Seriously sitting through a four-hour exam in my worst subject would be better than this awkwardness. I don't get it. We talked, it's not like we were strangers. Yet, here I am sitting in his truck, him driving down the highway in complete silence. Why did he have to call me kid?

"How's school going?" Reed asks and I look over to see that he, too, is feeling all this awkwardness.

"Fine," I say and turn to look out the window.

"How's dorm life?" He tries again.

"Fine," I say, not even looking at him this time.

"How are the boys at school treating you?" he asks.

What I really want to say is better than you, but I'm not brave enough. Not to mention our kiss in high school. How petty would I sound to bring up our whole three seconds? Even if they are all I think about before I go to sleep every night.

"Fi—well, actually better than fine. There are so many, I can't just have one." His eyes pop at my words and I feel empowered by his reaction. "You know how it is—can't settle too long." His eyes change and I see he's catching on to my lie. "Sorry," I continue, "I'm not like *you*. I didn't go away to school and live alone for the hook ups—yes, I've heard all about your, ah, relationships from Derek. I'm only focusing on school."

"Well, aren't you just fricking sunshine and roses," he says and I don't have to see him to know he has a smirk on his face. Is he relieved? Or is Reed enjoying my hostility.

Well, two can play that game. "How's Marissa?" I ask, trying to take the pressure off me.

"She's great," he says and that only makes me feel worse. I don't actually want to hear about them. "She's just not with me anymore."

My mouth drops open. "I'd say I'm sorry, but well, you know I don't like her," I say honestly and Reed chuckles at me.

"Could I expect anything less from you? You and Danni call her slutbucket. Who knew you'd be right and I'd catch her with one of my roommates," he says with a smirk, telling me he's not hurt by her actions. Maybe it wasn't as serious as I made myself believe.

"Ouch. You dodged a bullet there, Reed. You deserve so much better than a slutbucket," I say with a wink and we both burst out in a fit of laughter.

"So, how are things, really?" he asks, still chuckling and I feel compelled to tell him.

"Well, I was seeing the quarterback of the Longhorns."

He stops laughing and just stares at me. "You're just fucking with me right?" Reed says stone-faced.

"Ah. No, I was seeing Daniel Timberman." I had gotten used to this from other people as football is a big thing here and, well, that means Daniel is the most important thing to many. "Can you not go all crazy about it? People were weird about me dating him. It's like he's a celebrity or something," I say with a huff. Turning, I look out the window watching the trees whip past us as we continue on our drive.

"Was seeing or dating? Those are two different terms. Does Danni know?" he says in a stiff tone.

"Danni knows," I say, trying to avoid anything else, but unable to stop myself from glancing at him.

"She never told me." His fingers wrap around the steering wheel causing them to go white.

"Well, it's not like she's going to come out and say it. I'm sure she didn't keep it from you." Hoping my words will soothe him, I continue. "It's—"

"She *did* keep it from me," he interrupts and my head is spinning. I hate being on the spot like this. Never during high school had I gone to talk to Reed about guys. He always got annoyed or seemed uninterested, so when Danni would talk about them with him I just didn't join in.

"Maybe she just didn't think you'd be interested to know."

"I ask her, okay?" he says and his eyes connect with mine. For a second I see the Reed from that night, so many summers ago, but he quickly hides him away again.

"Oh, okay." What else do I say to that? He is coming off as an ass and it's only making me want to be quieter. Can't we just be the people we used to be? No, of course not. We have to grow up and make shit complicated. Lovely.

"Dating or was seeing?"

"I guess that depends on which one of us you ask, Reed," I say turning away from him.

"I'm asking you, Riley."

My eyes close and I take a sharp breath. He said my name. It's been years since he's called me that.

"Riley?" he says, snapping me out of my moment.

"Was seeing," I say and I turn to see his fingers relax against the wheel. "Danni didn't tell you because it's not serious." He gives me a stern look and I correct myself. "It *wasn't* serious, Reed. If it were, I would have mentioned him to you in our emails. I'm just doing what every other freshman does. Test the waters."

"You're not every other freshman." His words wrap around me and I almost let myself believe he means it in an endearing way and not like I'm another little sister of his.

"Yes, Daniel said the same thing after I told him I wasn't looking for anything serious when he wanted to make it so," I say and he throws his head back in a fit of laughter.

"Wait. So Longhorn's starting quarterback wants *you* to settle down with *him* and you tell him there are too many fish in the sea to settle for one right now?" Reed says, continuing to chuckle.

"Well, yeah—sort of. Without the use of fish," I say and start laughing with him.

"Wow, I bet that's not something he's used to hearing, especially from a naive freshman. Way to go easy on his ego."

Just like that my laughter dies.

Why can't he just look at me for who I am? No, I will always be a kid and naïve to him. Someone who needs to be protected and clearly from him because I can't take the whiplash my heart is getting from him. Maybe I'm reading too far into things, but I just feel like I see a possibility with us and then we are back at this.

I shift my gaze out my window trying to hide the tears of hurt and frustration gathering in my eyes. When will I really protect myself against this man?

I feel his hand wrap softly around my wrist, then he suddenly pulls away as if regretting his action. That stings more than any of his words have.

"So kid, are you excited for the cruise?" he asks and I lose it.

"Stop it," I spit out, trying to regain a semblance of calm.

"What are you talking about, kid?"

"Stop. Calling. Me. Kid," I say slowly so he doesn't miss it. "Maybe to you I will always look like a kid but trust me when I say Daniel didn't look at me like that and neither have the guys at school." It is like word vomit. "Just because you can't see me as anything other than a kid, doesn't mean that the men out there don't appreciate me and want me in their life. I'm not fifteen anymore, so wake up and smell the freaking coffee."

"Trust me, I know, all right," he says while shaking his head. Reed's eyes take in my appearance causing me to feel exposed.

"Can you just call me Riley? Treat me the same as all your sister's other friends. That's all I ask," I beg hoping he will finally just be normal around me again.

"I can't do that. Calling you Riley, I can do, but treating you like all my sister's friends, I can't do. I'm sorry."

Why did I think it could all be normal? At least he is going to call me Riley, but I wish we could just go back to a time when things felt easier between us. "It's a start, but I wish that night never happened; then you could just treat me like any other girl Danni brings around," I say so softly I'm not sure he hears me.

"Don't say that, because I don't."

Before he can say anything my phone lights up and he glances down at it, seeing Daniel's name pop up on the screen. I quickly ignore the call, hoping it won't bring up an argument again. Keeping Daniel from him wasn't a purposeful thought or idea. My mind just never processed that he might actually care about my life outside of his duties as my best friend's big brother.

"I wasn't acting like that about Daniel because he's like a celebrity."

I can't move. My body feels like it's paralyzed.

"Do you know why I call you kid?" Reed continues and I don't nod. I don't want to hear it. "It's not what you think."

"I doubt it," I say hastily.

"K.I.D...Keep it decent," He says slowly. My head turns to him and my eyes open wide in shock. "I told you it wasn't what you thought."

CHAPTER THREE

Imagine I freaked out…

"Keep it decent?" I repeat. "Pull over. Now!" I add firmly and he quickly maneuvers the truck off to the shoulder.

When it has barely come to a complete stop, I push out of the truck and begin pacing back and forward on the side of this busy highway.

"Are you going to be sick?" Reed is standing beside his open door. His face looks like he wants to ask more but I just can't think straight.

"Keep it freaking decent," I exclaim and he just nods his head at me while I continue on my path up and down the side of the truck.

"Riley, get your ass back in the truck. We shouldn't be out here with all this traffic. This is only supposed to be for emergencies, not your little girl meltdown."

That does it. I snap. There's no going back from the insanity that has taken over my mind.

"Little. Girl. Meltdown," I say and begin pulling my school sweater over my head, leaving me in a T-shirt. Reed's eyes spring wide open but I don't stop. Bringing my hand down to the hem of my T-shirt I lift it over my head, leaving me in a tank top with one of those built in bras. "I am *not* a little girl. I. Am. Not. A. Kid," I say and begin undoing my jeans button and then I yank down the zipper. "Do I look like a little girl?" I yell and just as I'm going to slip my hands over my hips to slide my jeans down to show him my womanly curves, Reed is in front of me.

"He just left." I cried and Danni was beside me in a moment. "He didn't even say goodbye. Just left this stupid letter."

"He may be my brother, but he's an asshole. I can't believe he'd kiss you like that and just leave. What a stupid jackass."

I would have laughed if I didn't feel like last night was the biggest mistake of my life. "I shouldn't have let it happen. This will change everything," I said between sniffles. "I'm an idiot."

"No, you are not. He's the only idiot here. I've been waiting for him to make a move on you for a while and he does it like this. I'm going to kill him," Danni yelled and I'm taken aback by her words.

"He liked me?"

"Well, now I'm not sure. Even if he does, he doesn't deserve you after this crap. You should call him and be all like 'what the hell, fucker?'" She said the last part in a sarcastic tone.

"But then I will be some desperate high school girl trying to get her crush's attention." Honesty with Danni had always worked best. She's the better of us two at it and sometimes her honesty is brutal.

"Well, that's exactly what we are. High school girls and I know you've had a crush on my brother since forever. He just needs to get his head out of his ass and notice that you're the best thing for him."

Her words hit home. As much as I wanted to call him, I wouldn't.

"Maybe he's waiting for you to get a hold of him," she added.

"No, he would have said that. He said he hated leaving me behind and that's exactly what he did. Reed has gone off to college, to date college girls who will have adult bodies too. I'm no match for that. He's moved on, so will I."

Even though I said I would move on, I knew I wouldn't. There was no moving on from Reed Humphrey. He was the guy girls dreamed about. I knew because he haunted my dreams many times. Now that I've gotten a taste, I know it will only be worse. Now I knew what I would be missing.

"Stop thinking so low of yourself," Danni insisted. "Every guy in school knows you're beautiful. What makes you even more gorgeous is that you don't even know it. You aren't that girl flaunting her tatas for everyone to see, just to get some attention and a quickie."

I couldn't hold it in and I broke out in laughter with her giggling right beside me.

Once we settled down, she placed a piece of my hair behind me ear and looked right into my eyes. "You are the girl guys want for the long haul."

"If I say 'just not for Reed', does that make me pathetic?" I asked shyly and she smiled.

"No, it only furthers what I'm telling you. Even though he doesn't deserve to cross your mind, you still care. Because you are Riley Dunham and you can't be anything else but the sweet, kind and caring person I love. He will wake up one morning and realize he's the one making the mistake."

"Hopefully it will not be too late," I said quietly, lowering my head.

Danni brought her finger under my chin, lifting my face so that I was making eye contact with her. "You could just go to the same university as him and show him what he fucked up."

I was already shaking my head in response before she'd gotten everything out. "No, I'm going to Austin. Close enough that if he still has a sliver of feelings for me it will kill him, and far enough away I don't look desperate. Besides, if he pisses me off, I'm a Longhorn and will shish kebob him," I said without a hint of sarcasm in my tone.

Danni slapped me on the back, startling me. "That's my girl."

In that moment, I knew I would have to protect myself against this man. If I was supergirl, he was my kryptonite—and not the fun red kind that just made me a badass, but the green kind that sucked the life right out of me.

Protect yourself, I remind myself but I can't think straight with him holding the zipper of my pants, having him pressed up against me. Thinking about that night. The hurt, everything he put me through each summer after that.

"I'm not a kid," I say because it's the only thing on my mind. The only thing I've ever wanted him to see.

His mouth crashes down on mine and he puts his hand around the back of my head, leaning me back so he has full access to my mouth. I'm stunned, and at first I don't respond.

I push him away and he just looks at me. His breath is labored and I can feel his hot breath against my cool skin.

"Fuck it," I say and grab him by the shirt, pulling him back down to me. I can't even think about it because he has pulled me up against him with the same hand wrapped around my head again and the other one slipping down my back to the hem of my pants. When his hand slips in the back of my jeans and I feel his fingers against my skin, I deepen the kiss, opening up to him. He doesn't miss a step and is with me step for step.

There is a honk and I clue in that people are driving by, seeing me in undone jeans and a skimpy tank top.

Reed pulls me behind the truck, hiding us from the traffic while never breaking apart from me. When I feel the truck press against my back, I wrap my arms around his neck and pull myself up to his height while wrapping my legs around his waist. I can't help but notice his reaction to this moment pressing against me. It only furthers my need to be close to him.

He pulls back and I wonder if it's over, just like before. "I know you're not a damn little girl. Every time I said kid it was to remind myself that you deserved to have a normal high school experience; I tried to give you that. If I could have claimed you for myself, I would have, but I never wanted you to regret being with me while I was away. People could have been upset because of our age gap and I didn't want you to ever regret a second with me," he says so fast I almost miss it.

"My only regret was not calling you after you left."

His mouth is on mine again and I feel the pull. It's like he takes me away from reality. We end up in our own little world where all the screwed up past isn't in the way.

I pull back from him enough to speak. "If you had have called I wouldn't have been able to keep myself away from you. I still can't."

The shy girl he knows is gone. My hand drifts down his chest as I kiss him until my fingers meet the buckle of his pants. Quickly I undo them while unzipping his jeans. The whole time he has me pushed against the back of his truck. I slip my hand in his pants and find him ready and waiting for me. If it isn't for the fact that we are on the side of road, I don't think I could stop myself. Slowly I bring my hand around him, gripping him with just the right amount of force. He quivers beneath me and I slowly slide my hand up and down while moving my body against him.

My body feels like it's going to overheat from all the contact I'm getting from him. Both his hands are now cupping my bottom under my jeans and I can feel his fingers sweeping across my lace panties. "You have to stop Riley," he says slowly and I almost do.

"Why?"

"Because if you don't, I'm going to blow right here on the side of the road." I feel him trying to push me down, with his hands sliding around to my hips, but I lock my legs around him and quicken my hand against him. It isn't long until he's groaning and putting his head into my shoulder while he gasps and I feel him come undone against me.

Once he is calm, I slide down and just look up at him. "Oh, you've made a mess of yourself," I say, then biting my lip trying not to laugh at him.

"Oh, you think that's funny, do you?" Reed says and he tries to push me against the truck again but I worm my way out of his grasp and dart into the overgrown grass beside the road. He just looks at me like he's going to pounce on me at any moment; I'm like a mouse caught in the cat's trap.

Outrunning him isn't an option, but I want to try now.

"If I have to catch you it's only going to be worse, Riley," he says and I almost walk back to him, but then he jumps towards me and I yelp. It isn't long before he's right behind me but I don't give up. We probably look like losers and the cops are going to show up any minute thinking this is a domestic issue. The thought of that makes me giggle and I feel him tug on my loose jeans. He falls and takes me down with him. Twisting around and landing on him with a thump, I can't help but smile at him. My fingers find their way to his hair and I run my fingers through it until he pulls me down to him. I gently kiss him, trying to savor this moment.

"Now I have to change. I might just have to punish you later for this, Riley," he says with a wicked grin on his face.

God, I hope so. I don't say anything, but giggle and pull away from him, helping him up. When he gets to the truck, he hops up into the truck bed, grabbing a change of pants and then jumps down. He opens the back seat and just smirks at it.

"Not going to happen," I say, smiling.

"We will see about that. For now, I will let you get away with defying me," he says jokingly. He is barely in there a minute and he's out in fresh jeans.

"All Clean?" I mock and he smirks at me, causing me to giggle. "Your fault for making a mess." I wink and now he's laughing with me.

"You're evil, you know that?" he teases as I go to get into the truck. He stops me and opens the door for me, lifting me up into the seat. He kisses me again and I melt. This man has so much power over me and he doesn't even know it. My hands pull him against me and the kiss becomes more intense. He slowly pulls away, showing it's just as hard for him as it is for me to stop this. Bending down, he tosses in my clothes that I'd taken off to prove a point. Reed just shakes his head and shuts the door, running around to his side of the truck.

I quickly pull my shirt back on over my tank. He jumps in and starts the truck then looks over at me.

"Wow," I say, still breathing heavily.

He brings his hand up to his mouth then smirks at me and I can't help but smile. "Wow, is right."

CHAPTER FOUR
Imagine I pretend…

It's dead silent as we continue their drive. "Wow" was all I could say. Not because I didn't enjoy our encounter, but because now my head is spinning. What the heck does this mean now?

Reed just keeps glancing over at me and I want to blurt out all my questions, but I know I can't act like the desperate high school girl he had first kissed a few years ago. It was innocent before, just a kiss. Now we have actually fooled around and it's something I know I won't ever forget. My years of haunted dreams had nothing on the actual experience of touching Reed. This man has damned me for the rest of men.

What was I thinking? How could I do that with Reed and *not* think it would mean a world of changes for me? Danni is going to kill me.

"Riley…" Reed says, taking in a deep breath.

I cringe. Here it comes.

"I think—"

I cut him off, not wanting to hear a letdown. "I must have needed that. Sorry, I kind of attacked you. You know how it is, when you have that itch you gotta have scratched," I say jokingly, trying to play this off like it meant nothing. That is the only way we are getting ourselves out of this without awkwardness.

"An itch," Reed says, nostrils flaring.

Looking out the window I try to keep myself composed and just go with it. "Well, I guess, technically, I was looking to take care of someone else's itch, but it sounds right to me. I don't mean that it wasn't fun, because, well, obviously it was amazing. But it is what it is," I say nonchalantly, never looking back at him.

"It is what it is?," he repeats and I close my eyes tightly at his tone.

Why did I think I could try to play this cool? All I did was make myself look like one of those girls who gets around. That thought makes me angry, though. *He* is that guy who gets around. I know this, based on the reports I get back on his college antics. It only infuriates me more because, who the hell is he to judge those girls?

"Let's not pretend you don't have your hook ups." I tell him. "Don't judge me because I wanted a little fun when we both know you were getting some when you weren't with Marissa. Maybe even when

you *were*," I say a little meanly, defensively, turning to him. "Don't act like I'm being ridiculous. We *all* do it."

"Get in the back now," he orders and I still.

Crap, I went too far. My anger got the better of me, putting me in this situation now.

"I'm sorry," I say shyly, hoping the glare he is giving me will soften but it doesn't.

"Now, Riley," Reed says and the way he says my name makes me flinch but quickly I undo my seat belt and climb into the back, doing up my new seat belt.

Great, he doesn't even want to be near me. Taking a peek, I see the white of his knuckles as he tightly holds the steering wheel. He is staring straight ahead and even though he's fuming, my heart can't help but feel for him. I can still see that vulnerable boy I met even though before me is a confident man that any woman would want. I see all of him. Not just how out-of-this-world sexy he is, but his heart and soul too. When I look at him, I see the real Reed Humphrey, not just the person he lets the world see.

Reed exits the highway and continues driving until we are pulling into a run-down stone parking lot that has a rusted carpool sign. My heart quickens. He's going to either tell me to get out or yell at me. Getting tossed in the middle of nowhere sounds better than him yelling at me. When the truck stops, he gets out and begins running his hands through his hair and I can tell he's frustrated. He starts kicking the stones causing some dust to kick up in the air. My hand goes to the door handle but I can't make myself open it. I've never seen him this angry, not with me at least. He either ignored me or made small talk in the last few years.

Suddenly he turns and sees me looking at him. My head shoots down and I put my hands in my lap, locking my hands together. The truck door opens on the other side of me and I feel the breeze. I do not look up, I can't. I'm frozen. The door slams behind him and I feel him sit on the bench seat.

"How could you say that shit?" he says softly. "You, of all people."

"So, I can't be like you or the rest of the world who hooks up because they want to. Oh right, I'm a child still," I say sarcastically and his hand reaches out, touching my thigh.

"Not that shit. I know you're not like the rest of the world, remember," he says and I can't help but feel he still thinks of me as that naive girl he kissed summers back.

"That was a long time ago, Reed. I'm not a little girl anymore."

He just stares at me for a moment. "I know you're not a fucking little girl," he murmurs after he pulls his hand off my thigh.

I blush and suddenly his face changes and I can't get a read on him. He has his eyes locked on me and I cower under his gaze. My phone rings and, welcoming the distraction, I go to reach for it but he stops me.

His eyes connect with mine. "Let it ring."

"It could be important, I do have people in my life other than you," I blurt out.

"Oh, I know, and that's the damn problem, isn't it?"

A look of confusion comes over my face. "Oh, so you can go and get your rocks off, but a girl has to be waiting for a guy. I'm supposed to sit and sulk over you for years because of one kiss in high school?"

"Well you did, didn't you?" he says with this satisfied smirk.

I smack him across the face, hard. My hand comes over my mouth in shock. What have I done?

His face hardens and I push myself right up against the door, trying to find the handle. I'm doing everything to push him away, when all I really want is to get closer to him.

He grabs my hand, the one that is trying to find my escape, and leans into me. "You can pretend all you like that you didn't want me all those years, just like I pretended all those years not to fucking want you."

As soon as he says it, he's kissing me again, reminding my mouth, my body, that I want him. At first I don't know what to do. My mind is spinning, but when I feel his hand slip under the hem on my shirt, making contact with my hip, I come alive under him. His mouth is divine. I've been kissed before but something about him makes his kisses feel so much…more. It's like I'd never really been kissed until now.

His lips leave mine and he trails kisses along my neck. "You aren't some fucking hook-up," he says, continuing to kiss my neck as he moves his hand up higher, coming right under my breast. "I know you, Riley. That kiss meant something." His hand moves under the cup of my tank's inbuilt bra and he brings his mouth back to mine briefly before pulling away slightly, his lips resting against mine. "*This* means something," he says, touching my bare breast.

I moan out lous as he begins caressing it. His mouth dips down and his tongue sweeps in at that moment, only intensifying everything I'm feeling.

His phone begins ringing but he doesn't move. It stops, but as soon as it does mine begins to ring again. Someone was trying to contact both of us.

Reluctantly, I tell him: "I don't want to stop but I have to check it. I'm sorry."

He doesn't pull away. He just moves his mouth further down my neck as I reach to grab my phone.

I don't even look at the caller ID. I just answer it. "Hello."

"You whore," Danni says and I jump slightly, causing Reed to chuckle against my neck. Clearly he can hear her.

"Hey Danni," I say, trying to ignore her comment. It could mean anything. She can't see us so she doesn't really know. Just as I try to sit up, Reed tugs me down and his hand starts undoing my jeans while his other hand remains on my breast.

"Don't hello me. I call you and you don't answer. So I call my brother and he doesn't, either. Now you finally answer sounding all breathless. Ugh, you whore," she says, sounding angry but I know she isn't. I don't think she really believes I'm doing what I'm doing right now—I don't even believe it. "Here I am at the airport, snowed in, and you are fucking my brother."

His hand slips into my panties, and I feel his fingers slide into me and I have to bite my lip not to moan.

"I wouldn't say we're fucking," Reed says, and I still, "but I'm working on it."

"What!" Danni screams and my eyes go wide at Reed. "Ew…Reed…"

"We are *not* having sex," I say and he pushes his fingers into me a little hard, causing me to groan.

"Oh. My. God," Danni whispers.

"I have to go," I say quickly and hang up the phone.

"Good choice," Reed says as he starts stroking me. My head drops back and I find myself spinning out of control against him.

"Reed," I moan and his mouth moves up to mine again.

"Let go Riley," he whispers and just like that, my body finds an incredible release. One I will never forget.

CHAPTER FIVE

Imagine I listened…

Zipping up my jeans and doing up the button, I can't look up at Reed. I know he's watching me but I just can't glance up at him. There is so much I want to say and I feel like I'd just blurt out everything in my head, and that would be horrid. He'd be overwhelmed. Heck, *I'm* overwhelmed.

"Riley?"

I don't move. I don't know what to say or do. Reed's hand comes under my chin and brings my head up so that I can look into his eyes. The blue eyes looking back at me are all that it takes. My eyes get glossy but I do not cry. It takes everything in me to hold myself together, but I do it.

"What's wrong?"

"Nothing," I say quickly and try to put a smile on my face.

His hand drops and his eyes look to the seat. "Well, something is wrong with me."

His words confuse me until the horror hits me. He is talking about what we've just done. Kissing me, touching each other. It was all a mistake to him.

"It was a mistake?" I ask questioningly, but from the look on his face I don't think he understands.

"Oh."

"Well, wasn't it? Is that what you are trying to tell me?" I ask softly, trying to keep my emotions in check.

Reed glances at me, stunned for a moment, then slowly moves towards me, kissing me lightly on the lips. "My only mistake was leaving you in Michigan. None of this was a mistake. I just don't know what you're thinking and it's killing me. Usually I can see right into you and I can't get a read on you. It's like you learned how to shut me out and I'm not used to it. It's like there is this protective bubble around you

keeping you from me," he whispers once he pulls away from me.

"You taught me that."

"I know I was a complete jackass. The way I treated you when I came back that summer and the following summer…I can't say sorry enough. When I saw you had moved on and just forgotten about a night I had played in my head a hundred times, I just figured you deserved to have what you wanted. I let you be a normal high school girl. I had to keep reminding myself that what I wanted didn't matter." He grimaced. "Keep. It. Decent. Calling you kid was how I reminded myself that I needed to do this for you. The other girls were distractions, which failed miserably because you are so beautiful and smart and my dream girl, and yet every guy wanted your attention. I had to start staying away from you because watching it drove me insane. Then Derek beat my ass before I left two summers ago and told me not to come back unless I was ready to treat you the way you deserved. So I went to school and tried to move on."

He puts his hands through his hair and I feel for him. Reed is putting it all on the line here and I don't even know what to say right now. "Meeting Marissa, and eventually dating her, was to get over this…you. I knew you'd be taking off to school. I didn't have the right to ask you to come to Houston with me or to be with me and give up your university experience. Something happened though—not just her being the wrong girl for me or the cheating. On my part, I promise I never cheated, physically at least. She may have physically cheated, but when she said she wanted to try again, I couldn't help but feel she wasn't the only one stepping out."

Reed takes my hand in his. Bringing it to his lips, he softly kisses the top of my hand. "Emotionally, I was never there. It was this girl from back home who I'd think about, dream about each night. She was the one I wanted to be with. So I came home for the summer ready to do whatever that girl wanted even if it destroyed me."

His eyes look away from me and I want to go to him, but I don't. "I get home only to find out that me being a complete asshole to her for years finally did it. She left and was going straight to university…elsewhere. I wouldn't get to see her and tell her everything I'd been holding in for so many years. Danni must have known what was going on because she continually made comments to me about my behavior, and I just sat there taking each hit. Fuck, I almost died when she told me you were going to Austin. I'd wished you would have been farther away, at least I wouldn't have been tempted. You have no idea how many damn times I almost got in the car to come here. Then this birthday celebration fell in my lap and I jumped on it."

He softly smirks at me, begging me to say something but I can see he's worried I'm either going to go all mushy on him or freak out.

I consider my reply, what tact I should take. "I was just protecting my sweetness, Mr. Humphrey. You know—the advice you gave me before you left for school. You didn't have to go all high school girl on me," I say with a devilish smirk on my face.

He glances at me like a wolf that has just caught a delicious lamb. His hands grab me, pulling me to him and he kisses me. At first, it's soft and gentle but something changes and he deepens the kiss. It's like every emotion is coming through to coalesce at this moment.

When he pulls away, he smiles softly at me, brushing a strand of my hair behind my ear slowly. "I meant it all," he says as he places a hand on each side of my face. "Every damn word."

"It's just—" I start.

"No, no 'just.' I was wrong. You put yourself out there for me and I ran, scared, like a little pussy. I don't know what I'd do without your smart mouth and that beautiful mind in my life. This past summer the only reason I didn't come find you was because Danni wouldn't tell me where you were. Bribery didn't even work, I told her I'd take her for a visit. She saw right through me."

I'd have to talk to Danni about this. Why didn't she tell me? Knowing Danni, she was protecting me. Maybe I *should* still be protecting myself from him. "I should call Danni back. She said something about flights cancelled."

He reluctantly agrees. Grabbing my phone I press her contact and she picks up on the first ring.

"Riley Dunham, you have some explaining to do," she says in a tone I just can't peg.

"I was just messing with you, Danni." Trying to save face might be the best option here. I don't even know what's happening here with Reed.

"Try again."

"I'm not a magic eight ball, you can't just shake me to get a different answer," I say jokingly and I feel Reed chuckle against me.

"I don't need one to know you're lying to me. If I was there I could see your tonsils, you are smiling so big," she replies.

"I don't have tonsils," I say smartly, causing Reed to snort.

"Just remember, you can outrun me now, but once we get on that cruise there won't be anywhere to run to. If we can *ever* get a flight out of here," she says, clearly irritated.

"What happened?" I ask, trying to change the subject.

"We are snowed in. Looks like we won't be meeting you at the hotel. Oh, and on that note, I called to cancel Mom and Dad's room, but there was nothing to cancel. I guess they lost *all* our reservations and are fully booked. So, Reed?" She waits for him to respond.

"What's up, sis?" he answers.

"Find a new hotel, and can you maybe *not* screw my best friend? I'd like to have her in my life and you are a complete asshole. Now go away. I want to talk to the person I love, not the loser trying to bone her," she says jokingly, but I know she's not kidding about her brother's behavior. His attitude towards me those two summers had caused a rift in them that hurt my heart because I was the reason behind it. No matter what, I wouldn't let that happen again. Even if it meant having to push away Reed.

"Yes, Danni. Don't worry, I will handle it," he says.

Danni pressed on. "Now, I'm sure he can still hear me, and I don't care. Girl, what the hell happened? Don't tell me you didn't do…you know…because I heard noises I don't need to hear when my brother is the one making you make them."

Danni and I have talked about sex and such before, but she's right; it is weird now, with it being her brother. "We haven't had sex."

Reed slides his finger up my thigh and mouths "Yet."

My heart stops and I shake my head, making him stop. He just chuckles, but my mind is racing. Having sex with Reed is something I've dreamed about. I know he's only joking—at least I think he is. If I said no, he wouldn't push it.

"Yeah, okay, so you haven't done it yet."

Reed mouths "See?" to me in response to her yet and I want to laugh.

"Riley, you know what I mean. What about everything we've talked about?"

Before she can say anymore, I need to get a handle on this conversation. There are things I don't want Reed hearing that Danni might say. "I had an itch, okay? He helped me with it. End of story."

"Oh, we are back to that itch again?" he says with a knowing grin on his face.

I swat him away and focus my attention back on Danni.

"If you say so," she says, somewhat skeptically, "but if he can't keep it in his pants, I might have to have someone 'take care of it.'"

I laugh at her response. She tells me that she has to go and figure out flights.

As soon as I hang up I look to Reed and he just laughs. "Oh shit, she's going to castrate me. I didn't really think long term when I was teasing her on the phone."

"Do you ever think long term, Reed Humphrey?" I say, laughing.

"With you, I do."

Complete. Silence.

CHAPTER SIX

Imagine I just went along with it…

Reed asked me to drive so he could look up places in Galveston on his phone. So here I am driving his truck along the highway. However, there is way too much going on in my head to be able to concentrate on the drive. Reed has called a few hotels but they seem to be all booked up. Finally he seems to be getting somewhere with the place he is currently on the phone with.

"That would be perfect, thank you," he says and hangs up the phone. "Okay, we are all settled. I booked us in at a place called Windswept. Every-

where else seemed to be booked." He smiles proudly and I can't help but return the smile.

"We should be there in about twenty minutes, so put the hotel's address in the GPS and it will lead us right there," I say and Reed grabs the device, doing exactly that.

It isn't long before we are pulling up in front of our accommodation and I realize it isn't some hotel like a Comfort Inn. It's a cute little Bed & Breakfast. If things with Reed weren't so complicated, I'd almost be excited, but my stomach is in knots just thinking about this. I pick up my phone and search this place while Reed gets our bags. It says the house is old and had survived the hurricane in the nineteen hundreds. I continue reading and my door opens. Looking up, I see Reed watching me closely.

"You know there are rumors that this place is haunted, right?" I ask.

"No. Funny it didn't say that on its webpage," he says with a smirk. "Don't worry, I will protect you," he says.

"It's not the ghosts I need protecting from," I whisper as he helps me out of the truck.

"What was that?" Reed asks and I panic at the fact he might have heard me.

"I said I'm not the one who's going to need protecting," I say slyly. "We both know who the big baby here is. Don't worry, I will keep you safe and I could always ask them to keep a hallway light on for you."

"I hate you," he says, shaking his head at me.

"Oh, well, no more helping those itches then," I say and take off inside before he can catch me. As soon as I'm in I glance around and I'm speechless. This place is absolutely beautiful. It pulls at my heart that we are here under these circumstances. The whole house has either been beautifully restored or preserved well. There is a welcome area and a small woman stands there greeting guests. Once I approach her, I feel Reed's hand find the small of my back. The woman smiles softly and I can't help but feel drawn to her.

"Hello there, I'm Madeline. Are we checking in?"

I nod because something about her just makes me speechless.

"Yes, I spoke to you earlier on the phone. I'm Reed Humphrey."

Her eyes just keep looking between us, like she can see everything we are thinking in our heads. I hope not, because my head can't even navigate through this storm of emotions going on.

Madeline moves around her desk and selects a key for us. I just stare at it. One key? Oh crap, did he only book one room? Well, I guess he wouldn't exactly be far off to assume we could share, and this *is* a Bed & Breakfast—usually a venue for couples….

When Madeline sees me looking at the single key, I see her clue in. "Is something the matter dear?" she asks.

Reed notices my concern. "I didn't think. I'm sorry, Riley, it wasn't intentional." He moves his hand from my back to my hip and squeezes softly trying to convey his apology. "We need two rooms," he says, looking at her with his eyes looking bluer then I thought possible. I can see the sadness in them so much clearer.

"Oh dear, that is a problem. I only thought you needed the one room. I just sold the last room; I'm afraid we are fully booked," Madeline says and I see her trying not to look at me.

"Its fine. No problem, really," I say trying to put on the biggest smile I can to make Reed and this woman feel better. Reed seems to cheer up but I see her watching me closely, looking for the truth behind my words. "Thank you," I say to her before grabbing the key and going off in search of our room.

Together, just us. What have I gotten myself into?

Reed follows me and when we come across our room, I turn, giving him a shy smile and open the door. The room before us is like the rest of the place. Beautiful, old and elegant, like nothing I could have ever imagined. It's cruel, in a way, because this is what any girl would dream of if they were here with their boyfriend. I'm here with someone I *want* to be in my life in that role, but we are nowhere near those terms.

"Well, is it everything you thought it would be?" he says jokingly, nudging me.

Glancing around the room I put my hand to my face like I'm thinking and then turn to him. "Yes, it is. Except when I think of places like this, you aren't here," I say with a smirk.

"Ouch," he says, smirking at me, like he knows I'm kidding. "Very funny."

"Who says it was a joke?" I say in a serious tone and keeping my face in check so he doesn't see through me.

"Oh really?" Reed says. He starts to take a step towards me, until I am up against the bed. "Are you sure you want to play this game with me, Riley? I will win," he replies and my knees go weak from the grin on his face. It is pure desire and lust. He leans into me, causing me to fall back to the bed, but just before I hit it he catches me, bringing me down softly as he leans against me. I can feel how much he wants this by the way his hands are moving against my burning skin.

"Try me, Humphrey," I say boldly and I immediately regret my choice of words as he collides with my body and kisses me passionately as we fall onto the bed. His mouth locked against mine, the way he continues to move against me has my body in overdrive. My mind wanders to how many other girls have been blessed with this experience. His hand slips under my shirt and all thoughts of other people are gone. It's just Reed and Riley, like it should be.

When his hand finds its way under my tank top, I can't help the moan that escapes me. That action only furthers his excitement and there is no denying he wants this just as badly as I do when I can feel his arousal pressed against me. He's turned this moment around on me. I thought I was in control, but my body has betrayed me.

Pulling him tightly against me, I try to turn us over, knowing I won't be able to by myself but that he will assist me. Just as I predicted, he rolls over, taking me with him, and I am now straddling him. The only thing keeping us from touching on every level is our clothing. Just as I think it, I see him bring his hands to my pants, undoing them. All I do is watch, seeing how much control this man has over me.

He leans up and I know he's going to try and slip my pants down or move me so he can. *Wake up, Riley. Ball's in your court.* I push him down and he groans at me taking control. He closes his eyes, and lets his hands fall away from me, enjoying the power I am now taking from him.

Lifting my bottom up, I undo his pants and try tugging them down. He lifts up, allowing me to slide his jeans off, which I do with little trouble, taking off his socks and shoes too. Grabbing the hem of his shirt with his help, I pull it up and off, leaving him in just his boxers. I lean down, kissing him, and run my hands along his bare chest, causing him to put his hands on my bottom, pulling me into him as I move.

Starting at his neck, I begin kissing my way down his chest, and out of his arm's reach. It's now or never.

Before he has a chance to stop me, I get up off the bed and act like I'm going to take my shirt off, but instead, at the last minute, I bend down, grabbing his clothes and dart for the door.

"I win, Reed," I yell as I open the door and run down the hall, past Madeline, with the button of my pants still undone and his clothing bunched in my arms.

"Riley," he yells from the doorway behind me and I just keep on running. We are either going to be kicked out or give the owner something to talk about.

CHAPTER SEVEN

Imagine we talked about it…

Sitting here, by the water outside the BnB, it's like the world has stopped. The sound of the lapping waves is all I hear. It's cold and I didn't bring my jacket, but I use Reed's jeans to sit on, and I pull his shirt over me to keep me warm.

I can't believe I'd done this. Gone this far with him and then bailed.

I don't even know what "this far" is. He tore me apart last time, when he didn't return, and I'm not sure I can deal with the loss again, if he woke up after our first night together and realizes he made a mistake. So, my actions ensured that moment never happened.

I'm a coward. I'm not sure I can look at Danni and be around the family in the future, having to see him be happy without me after all of this. Did I screw everything up, or was I just protecting myself, as he had taught me to?

Watching the waves roll in, I am surprised to realize he is now watching me, trying to get a feel for what is going on in this head of mine. I wish I knew, and then I'd know what to do next, but all I keep thinking is "I'm like these waves." I come in, every time, but I always have to leave. Their time at the shore is always limited, just like my time with Reed. The pull of the ocean will bring the waves back to their reality, like I am being pulled back to mine. I know this will all come crashing onto the shore, but will there be enough of me left to remain whole afterwards?

"Riley?" he finally says.

I don't turn to him. I just keep watching the waves, wishing they could carry me out to sea with them. I'm not ready to have this conversation. It will change everything because I can't hold back anymore. Trying to be this carefree girl is draining me when I feel this impending doom.

"Riles?" he says softly, bending down to me but not touching me.

The childhood name brings it all home for me. How much I can lose if I give in and screw this up; what I'd be without for the rest of my life. Sometimes having someone in your life in a limited way is better than not at all, right? But can we just keep laughing our way through this?

"Took you long enough," I tell him, trying to keep my tone light. "Thanks for the clothes."

"You know, you don't have to pretend. It's just you and me out here," he says quietly as he takes a seat next to me, still not touching me.

Before today, I only had a small kiss to think of, a stolen moment, but now I have touches that will haunt me for a lifetime.

"There's no one around but us, Riles."

"That's the problem though." I wish I could take this night back, because now I know there is no going back and we will have to talk about it.

"Did you not want this?" he asks, putting his hand on my leg and I pull it away.

"What is this?" I say, standing up, throwing my hands up in the air in frustration. "Is this just an itch and then it will be over? Are you just going to kiss—hell, do more than kiss—and then run again?" I yell at him and some nearby birds take off in flight.

"I thought I was pretty clear about my reasons for that," he says in a serious tone, turning away from me, staring out at the ocean.

"You know what I was thinking before you came?" He doesn't respond so I just keep going. Reed is always a risk because I never know what version of him I'm dealing with. "I wished I was a wave that never got to touch the sand. One that stayed far out in the ocean, away from land, because once it's touched the ground its time is limited. In the ocean it just seems less final. To me at least, it feels that if I never touched the sand, only to be pulled away again, I wouldn't know what I was missing," I say calmly, hoping to get my point across, but he doesn't move a muscle and that frustrates me. I grab a handful of sand, throwing it at his back, causing him to turn. "You're the freaking sand, Reed. My moment of limited joy that always ends. Like the waves, my moment is fleeting and I'm already being dragged back out to sea."

His eyes focus on me but he *still* doesn't move.

"I can't do this, Reed. I'm sorry, but nothing about what is happening between us is helping me. If anything, it's making me feel more helpless. It's like this big moment is coming and I can't help direct it or shape it. It's what I can do now that counts and who I am after that. That might mean a world without you because I can't just have these fleeting moments in time with you and go back to a world without the damn sand, when you ditch me again."

"Ril—."

"No. Don't, please. I can't deal with this right now. Not from you, because it will change everything." My heart is racing and it's like I can't catch my breath, but I know why. It's Reed. He has always had this effect on me, even when I've thought this through and practiced telling him everything. "On some level you're attracted to me. Back in high school that would have been enough for me, and what we've done would have been too. Now, after these past few years, it's too late. I know you liked what happened between us tonight, and I can't say I didn't either, but it's not enough for me. Because of that, I wish I could take it all back. Every touch, every kiss and every word except the ones that showed you were just my best friend's big brother and I was just a child."

"Other than those two damn summers of misperception, did I *ever* treat you like you were just a child to me?" he roars in frustration and I yelp, stepping back. Immediately, regret fills his face and he reaches out to touch me, but then changes his mind, putting his hand back at this side. "I explained why I was the way I was. I thought we both knew what this was and I'm sorry you thought different. We can forget this ever happened."

When he says that my heart drops, confirming why I had needed to protect my heart in the first place. Just like that, all those dreams I'd had of us being together are gone and I'm left with our limited memories. I now know I will be waking up tomorrow in a world I don't want to be in, but I have to live with my reality. Looking down, I see the pain in my existence. Sand, how will I ever look at it the same again?

Kicking the sand, I yell out at the waves that the sand I've displaced is now touching. "Stupid freaking sand. I need to find snow to cover all this shit up." Suddenly Reed begins laughing behind me and I turn, glaring at him. "You think this is funny, do you?"

"Actually, I do. You're wishing for snow to cover the sand. What is wrong with you? No one wishes for snow."

"I do," I say firmly.

"You are an idiot," he says seriously, and I can't help but get up, walk over to him, pushing him hard.

"Take that," I say childishly, knowing I am being petulant, but unable to help myself.

He chuckles at me, somewhat fondly, only furthering my rage.

"If you call me a child," I point out, "you won't have to worry about children, because I will make sure you can't have any. Got it?" I say glaring at him, my hurt from years past bubbling to the surface.

He continues to chuckle and I walk a few feet away in frustration, not trusting myself to *not* try pushing him in the water. If I thought I could, I would, but I'm sure I would be the only one ending up wet if I tried.

"I'm pretty sure I don't see you as a child, after tonight's events, so that was actually funny. I know why you did it, anyways: you were feeling vulnerable, so you pushed me. Riley, you may get older but certain things don't change. I actually like that. It means I know what to expect from you, even if that is the unexpected."

So, I'm predictably unpredictable, but he likes it. What the hell does that even mean? "Ugh," I groan in frustration.

"Do I have to spell it out for you? I know what is going on right now, but you are just letting it slip through the cracks," he says and he takes off a little ways up the beach, grabs a stick, and comes running back to me.

He begins drawing something in the sand but I can't see what as he's blocking it on purpose. "Now, when the wave touches it, the wave will be carrying my message out to sea. Meaning my words, my sand, will always be touching the water—always touching you. You don't have to wish to be that wave coming to shore anymore to get a taste of us, because as soon as you touched the sand, you took me back out with you."

He looks at me, his expression gentle, as I try to absorb his words, then continues on. "You still don't get what it's like to be me in this situation. I will try to describe it another way," he says, still covering what he's drawn in the sand. "I'm actually the water and you are the fucking moon. I can hold your reflection but never actually touch you. Do you have any idea how painful that is?"

He steps back and when I can see what he's written, my mouth drops open. I can't speak. I can't move. I just watch the wave finally come far enough up the shore to catch the words, carrying them out to sea to be with that wave forever.

You love me Riley, but most importantly I have always loved you.

CHAPTER EIGHT

Imagine he really did see me…

"What?"

That is all I can say as I watch the waves come up again, touching the fading words before me.

"There is no "liking" here, between us," he points out, gently. "It's been love for me, for a long time, if not since the day your freckled face pushed me out of the way when we first met. I love you, I love touching you too, but it's more than that," he says, taking a step closer to me with each of his words. "I've. Always. Loved. You."

When he's right in front of me, he reaches out for me but I take a step back. As I do, his face falls.

"You love me?" I ask, incredulous, needing the space to process.

"More than anything," he says, looking at me again.

"So you knew I loved you, all those years? You loved me then too?"

He nods and puts his hand on my face.

Quickly I kick him in the shin causing him to wince in pain. "I hate you."

"Should have seen that coming," he says with a half-smile on his face. Before I can kick him again, he grabs me, pulling me towards him and he kisses me hard, putting any thoughts I had out of my head. He softly tugs on my bottom lip and I bring my arms around him, pulling him as tightly against me as I can while we kiss.

He pulls away eventually, both of us panting, and my eyes are closed. When I open them, I see his triumphant smile.

"I still hate you," I say.

"I wouldn't have it any other way," he says, chuckling as he puts his arm over my shoulder, guiding me up the beach back towards the Bed & Breakfast.

Once we are at the top of the beach I take one final look out at the ocean and I still wonder if I will ever look at one the same way ever again.

"Riles?" Reed grabs my chin, bringing my face right in front of his. "I do love you. More than you will ever know. I'm not sure what all this means but I do know I love you."

I can't help the smile that comes to my face.

He grins widely at me, in return, a devilish twinkle in his eye. "You're not *just* some itch."

"Well, you were an itch for me. Doesn't mean I don't love you," I say to him, playfully.

His grin slips a little, but then he re-masks his vulnerability. It isn't until this moment that I really see him for what he is. That he cares just as much as I do about our future. Just like me, he took a risk in telling me something important, but then I joked, like we always did before, when our feelings threatened to get serious. It was our thing, but I now know my response was not the best one in this moment. We are growing up.

Turning into him, I place my face against his chest and all I smell is Reed, and it's like home to me. If I smelt that scent again, I would be able to tell it is him, without even opening my eyes. "Reed, you just came into my world and tore it apart. I was this shy thing from Alabama who talked funny and you didn't care. You helped me sound the same as all of the other kids, you never laughed when I slipped, or if I got angry and my southern ways came out. You protected me and you gave me the advice I needed to protect myself from you until we were ready."

He puts his hands softly into my hair. "I suspected then that I might have been something you'd need to be protected against. Saying those things to you and leaving you that night was like ripping out my heart and leaving it there with you. Yes, I dated other women and all that goes with that, but I still loved you—I just knew you weren't ready when I was. I knew that one day you'd either give me a chance or you'd find someone who took you away from me." He smoothed my hair back with one hand. "It was a waiting game for me. A dangerous one. My heart was already with you then and I didn't want it back. I still don't."

His words embrace me and I feel myself floating. I couldn't have dreamt of better words. They were more than I ever wished to hear.

"I know Daniel was someone you were seeing and that killed me, you have no idea. I don't need to know about your past. If you want to know mine that's fine, but if I had to write a list the only name I'd want on it would be Riley. The others meant nothing," he whispers in my ear.

"What about Marissa?" I ask and the jealousy coming from me is clear.

He laughs softly. "Still the jealous girl, I see. My answer is still the same. She meant nothing. She was a distraction and just me going through the motions. We both have pasts which we can't change. We either deal with it or let it ruin what we are creating between us." He pauses, before continuing. "Daniel still wants you, I am sure, but it comes down to what you want. I know what I want," he says, lowering his head into my shoulder, hugging me tightly like he's afraid to let go.

I push away from him softly and he lets me go. Turning away from him I look back out at the water. I never thought I'd have everything I could ask

for and not know what to do. There are things he's assuming that I should just let go, but I am honest to a fault when it comes to things of this nature. I needed to tell him of my past.

"Daniel wasn't anyone significant, either," I start out. "I've only kissed one other person in the same way I've kissed you. It was heated, to a point, but it's over. We haven't seen each other in a couple months, but we are still friends." I pause, almost imperceptivity. "I've never done it though," I say finally, never looking back at him.

"You kissed someone who you're still friends with?"

I can tell his understandable jealousy stopped him from hearing the rest of my words. "It's in the past, remember," I say.

"Right," he affirms. I feel him place his hands softly on my hips, pulling me into him so that my back is flush up against his chest, his arms sliding around my waist from behind.

I can tell he still hasn't clued in and I feel like I have to scream it. "I'm a virgin, Reed."

Suddenly, he spins me around, putting both his hands on my face and stares into my eyes. I know he's checking to see if I'm lying because I always do this twitchy thing on my face.

"It never felt right," I whisper and glance down at his shirt.

"How is that even possible?" he says and there is almost a sense of wonder to his tone. Asshole.

"It's not that I haven't had the chance. I almost did with someone else but I couldn't. I wasn't ready. It didn't feel right. There was too much baggage with this person. Too many people could get hurt by us being together, so we didn't."

I feel his grip on me tighten. "I wish I could say it doesn't bother me, but it does. I'm glad you told me, even though you didn't have to," he says and I know he's trying to rein in his jealousy.

"It wasn't right because it wasn't you, Reed," I finally say, glancing up at him and my eyes are full of tears. It takes everything in me to hold them in, to stop them from spilling over.

"Riles…" he whispers but I don't stop, I *have* to say this. I *have* to put it out there and just let the chips fall where they may.

"You didn't know it, back then," I start, a little self-consciously, "but I'd have done anything to keep you.

I know we have so much to learn and deal with, but all of that aside, that doesn't change the way you make me feel. You said I was the moon against the waves to you. Well, you aren't just the sand to me. You are the sun, the wind that makes the waves and everything in between. Without you I don't know what I'd do and that's what scares me, because I love you with everything in me and that means you have the power to take everything from me."

Finally the tears spill over and I don't bother trying to hide them. He brings his hand up, wiping them away and kisses me softly on my cheek. "It's a risk, but I'm willing to take it. I promise I will leave all those women in the past where they belong. Just like I wrote in that sand, it's always been you. The greatest loss would be you. Are you sure you are willing to give up your past, to finally start something with me?" he asks and I know he needs to hear it from me.

I need to tell him those moments with the other two guys are over and in the past; it's all about him.

"I promise I am here with you now. Daniel and Derek are in my past." As soon as I say it, I clamp my mouth shut and the tears start coming down faster because I realize what I have just done.

"Derek," he says, pushing me away from him.

I feel bereft at the disconnection between us, the force of his recoil almost knocking me down. It's like he just cut the cord holding us together and I can feel the sting acutely.

"My best friend?" he accuses and I flinch.

Reed turns and walks away, leaving me falling to the sand, wishing I was just a wave being taken out to sea.

CHAPTER NINE

Imagine I screwed it all up before it even started…

I stay down at the water's edge for over an hour. Reed doesn't come back. When the cold gets to be too much for me, I make myself walk back to the Bed & Breakfast, and to our room. Opening the door, I see that Reed isn't here and my heart drops. My phone rings and I rush over to it on the bed, answering it without looking.

"Reed," I say hopefully and when I hear the voice on the other end, my heart breaks.

"Rye, are you okay?" It's Derek and by the sound of his voice he knows exactly what's going on.

The tears that I thought had finally stopped start falling at an alarming rate. I'm sobbing and can't even answer Derek.

"I'm going to get on a flight and come get you okay? Everything will be fine." Derek's words calm me for a moment but then the overwhelming fear of him being here when Reed comes back takes over.

"You can't. Reed is here. He knows about us. I'm so sorry, I didn't mean to tell him." I hear Derek sigh into the phone and I feel dread overcome me.

"Reed isn't coming back. He called me, and to say he is pissed would be an understatement. I know you didn't tell him everything, but he got the point and there was no talking him down. I'm coming to get you, I'll rent a car and we will drive you home. Danni can't get flights out, so they've had to cancel the trip until the weather is better. There was no way they were going to make it out there for the cruise. Stay put and I will come to you, okay?"

Derek has always been saving me. Usually from Reed, but I never thought about it that way before. "Thank you, Derek. I miss you," I say honestly, because even with our past he has been my best guy friend for years.

"Don't worry Rye, we will get this sorted out. I miss you too, more than you know. I hate that you chose to move so far away," he says.

I can't help but feel torn. This is why I stopped things with Derek, because he could make me feel things that I wasn't sure I was ready for. Derek had chosen to stay in Michigan, until this year when he changed universities. He's so driven he graduated in three years instead of the four it takes most of us to finish college. He used to be at one of the other universities I had originally applied to but I had ultimately determined I didn't want to be with him or Reed. I needed to find me and make new friends.

Danni understood, but Derek was hurt when he found out. Reed never knew and now I doubt he cares how everything came about.

"Love you, Rye. See you soon," Derek says, like always.

"Love you too, Derek. Thank you."

He hangs up and I find myself looking around the room, unable to stay here. I see Reed everywhere. Grabbing my coat and purse, I finally notice that Reed's bags are indeed gone. Not bothering to lock the door I leave the room and go back outside to feel the ocean air again. It's the only thing that will help at this point.

Walking around, I notice the area has its local charm and historic buildings. I can't help but feel like this is my life. This place was ruined by a hurricane and now has beautifully grown into something more. I'm sure some things were ruined but out of it something new was able to start.

Out of the corner of my eye, I see Reed's truck parked at the local bar. "Just go in there," I say to myself and take off in that direction.

When I walk in I can smell stale beer and it almost turns my stomach. Okay, so this is *not* one of those local charms. After getting my stomach back in order, I look around but when I hear his voice, I stop. Turning, I see him in the back hall that leads to the bathrooms with some brunette pressed against the wall. By the way he's wobbling, I can tell he's drunk and I feel my lunch coming back up.

"Oh my God," I say and he pauses, looking at me. I see the hurt in his eyes and he looks like he is going to stop, but then something changes and he turns back into the brunette. My heart smashes on the floor.

For a second I feel the need to run but then something snaps inside me. "Hell no," I say, stomping over to them. "Beat it," I say to the woman, pulling her off him. She squeals before turning on me, but look at my face and the anger rolling off me, and she wisely takes off in the other direction.

"Seriously, you can fuck my best friend but I can't get a little tail?" he slurs and I slap him hard across the face.

"No, I didn't do that. If you listened, Derek and I never had sex. Daniel and I have never had sex. I've never had sex with anyone, because I wasn't ready. And when I look at you now…I know why I haven't." My disgust, my pain, is evident as I look at him. "Look at what you men do when you get pissed off. You hurt us. You couldn't just talk to me. No, you leave me alone and stranded and go find a piece of ass, like nothing between us ever mattered. So much for our pasts not mattering." I turn away, not wanting him to see the tears filling my eyes. "Go find your newest slutbucket. I'm done trying to prove my feelings for you. Maybe you should think about the fact that you caused this situation between me and Derek to happen, with you leaving me and calling me a kid, incessantly. Leaving it to Derek to console me. We never did it to hurt you, because I thought you didn't even care about me." I dash away frustrated tears. "You can't be a man-whore and think I'm not allowed to meet people too. I'm sorry he's your best friend but it happened and I can't change that."

I start to walk away he grabs my wrist, pulling me to him. He turns me around, trying to kiss me and I push him hard and he goes down.

"Are you kidding me?" I scream down at him. "I'm not something for you to toy with. I'm a person with feelings. Feelings for you that are killing me right now, so no, you don't get to treat me like crap because your ego is hurt. Go find the brunette and leave me the hell alone," I say, running out of the bar and bumping into the brunette as I push out the door. "He's all yours," I spit out and take off back to the Bed & Breakfast. I'm need to pack all my stuff and leave. I can't be here.

Running through the halls of the Bed & Breakfast, I hope no one sees me because I can't help the sobs that are escaping me now. Once I'm inside the room I just wanted to leave, but when I see Reed's discarded shirt, I can't help but grab it and go to the bed. I collapse there wanting nothing more than to let the world swallow me whole. Crying myself to sleep seems to be the best idea. It isn't long until I'm drifting away to a world that will now forever haunt me.

It's dark when I hear knocking at the door. Looking over, I see it is after midnight and I jump out of bed. Pulling open the door, I see him. He's wearing a plaid shirt and jeans that show off what I like about him. His hair is wet so it's either raining or he's had a shower. I can still smell the alcohol clinging to him, even though it appears he has sobered up.

"Happy Valentine's Day," Reed says, handing me flowers and I just stand there. He takes my lack of words as a green light, stepping into the room and closing the door behind him.

"What is this?" I say quietly, watching him as his eyes take me in and I can't help but feel the heat in me rising.

"I love you," he says and before I can do anything, he is leaning me down into the bed. His hands are rushed and shaking. The way they move over me has my body going in every direction. I want to pull away, but I want to be closer. It's a constant war with myself.

My emotions are everywhere but I don't pull back. I can't. I'm drawn to him in a way I can't explain. "I love you too," I say softly against his lips and he presses down against me, pinning me to the bed.

"I needed to hear that," he says, and I pull him by his hair, tugging his head up so I can see him. Looking into his eyes, I see all the pain of the past there. How sorry he is for everything that is happening, but I also see that he loves me.

A slight knock comes at the door and it opens. "Rye, I'm sorry to just walk in," Derek says and I still.

"Shit," I whisper and everything goes to hell.

CHAPTER TEN

Imagine I can't fix it…

"What the hell is he doing here?" Reed roars and I flinch, jumping off the bed in the opposite direction of both of them.

"I could ask you the same thing," Derek says calmly, never taking his eyes of Reed.

"You called him?" Reed accuses, turning to me.

"No, you called me and told me to shit bricks," Derek interrupts. "I called Rye because I knew you must have treated her far worse. You told me you left and I knew she was stuck here. Unlike you, that mattered to me." Derek says, pointing at Reed. "Don't blame this on her. If you could have handled your shit none of this would have happened, but, like always, you have to go balls to the wall and screw it all up."

Reed just glances between the two of us and I can't help but look away.

Derek continues. "Us, in the past? We didn't do it to hurt you man. I asked you about her, then I beat your ass when you talked trash. Neither of us knew what it meant and we called it quits when she went off to university in another state."

Reed glances at me while Derek is talking to him and I try to keep my eyes on him so he sees everything I'm feeling.

"We?" He asks and I go to answer but he turns to Derek.

"She broke it off; I didn't stop it. I wouldn't tie her down when she was just starting out." Derek says and I can't help that I turn to him. He might be able to hide it from Reed, but I can see it written all over him. Derek still has feelings for me. His eyes lock with mine and I feel everything he's trying to convey to me.

"None of this matters, Reed," Derek mutters, finally turning his gaze back to his friend. "It's over between us. I wasn't the one just kissing her—that was you. Drop it, man," he pleads and I feel for him. Derek never asked to see us making out, and he is being the better man here. I would have never done it if I thought he could walk in on us.

"That's right, I was here with her. I bought her flowers, I love her and will always love her. Can you say the same?" Reed demands.

Derek says nothing, he just glances at me.

Reed doesn't stop: "So she left you but you come here to get her when I screw up? Sounds like you're trying to get her back from me. Waiting for me to screw up and swoop in, stealing my girl."

I've had enough. "I was never your girl, Reed. I'm me. Riley, who can damn well talk for herself, got it?" I turn the full force of my frustration onto Reed. "You can't call me your girl when several hours ago you were pressed into some slutbucket after I'd just broken my heart open for you, telling you I loved you," I say and my voice is shaky.

It happens so fast I blink and nearly miss it. Derek tackles Reed, who didn't see it coming, and they are now punching the crap out of each other. Derek's fist goes hard into Reed mouth and I see blood on Derek's knuckle. I yelp and Derek's eyes dart to me, giving Reed a chance to capitalize on the situation. Reed punches him and Derek moves quickly so it's his shoulder that Reed connects with, but I can see it still causes Derek pain.

This is ridiculous. It won't solve anything and it won't change the past.

"Stop it. Stop it. Stop," I scream, tears running down my face, and they both stop and stare at me. "I'm not worth it."

Before they can say anything in response, I take off, running out the room and past the owner again. This woman is going to think I'm mental; I'm never going to be allowed back here. I don't stop until I'm away from any humans and down by the beach. Without thinking, I just walk into the water even though it's the middle of February and freezing. The cold water takes away the pain in my heart and numbs me. I go deeper and deeper until I have to swim to keep myself afloat.

I've never felt anything like this before. Why does it have to be this way? Why couldn't we just have had our chance back when it was less complicated? The waves begin to get stronger, pulling me deeper but I don't swim against them. I let them take me out further, away from the pain. Away from all the despair that is behind me. I finally can be one with the waves and go through the full cycle.

A massive wave overtakes me, pushing me under and I struggle to break the surface. I continue to struggle against the waves but I can't swim in. I'm frozen here and the numbness overtakes my entire body now. In the distance I can hear screaming but I'm too far out to know who it is.

Another wave comes and I am barely able to keep myself above the waterline. I break the surface again. The only thing I hear before the ocean takes me back under is people calling out. I can't struggle anymore, my body is cramping and shutting down. It's giving up.

"Riley," a voice screams out as I begin to give in to the water and numbness, letting the ocean take me out to sea.

CHAPTER ELEVEN

Imagine I put it all on the line...

"Breathe...Breathe, Riley," I hear in the darkness and then I feel like I'm being pulled forward. Like a rush of water smashing against the rocky shore.

My body expels the water my lungs have taken in and I continue coughing, while he holds me in his arms. "What were you thinking of, going out in that?" he says in agony and I can't look at him.

"I just wanted to be in the water. You know how much I love it. Then I got pulled in further and further and I couldn't move."

Turning, I see him, the guy who is always saving me, adding another rescue to his list. Pushing myself up, he holds me against him, trying to steady me, and I appreciate it.

"Maybe we should get you to a hospital," Derek suggests and I shake my head. Without thinking I lean forward and kiss him, at first softly but then I deepen it. He lets me lead and doesn't move past this moment. Putting in every emotion I can, I let him know he's not alone. I feel it too.

When I pull away he just stares at me knowingly. "This doesn't change anything," he states and I nod.

"I wish it did. You have no idea how much I wish it did," I say in a whisper, but I feel those words in every piece of my soul.

"Do you love me?" he asks shyly and I glance at Derek with new light. Never have I seen him this vulnerable and it tears at me that it is me doing this to him.

"Yes," I answer honestly.

"Are you truly in love with me, Rye?" he asks, again, wanting the truth.

Seeing him like this, I know I need to give him this. Even if it's not going to change anything, he deserves to know. "I am in love with you Derek, it's why I ended things. I was so confused between feeling love for both Reed and you. You make me feel things I never have before, that scares me more than anything." Putting my hand in his, I feel like this is it. It's now or never. "I will always love you, and I might be making the biggest mistake of my life right now, but if I don't try with Reed I will always wonder 'what if' and you deserve more than that. I love Reed and I love you," I say as the tears cascade down my cheeks.

"I want you to be sure. That's why I let you go before and it's why I'm going to do it again," he says with a deep sigh. "That's how much I love you, Riley. All I want is for you to be happy and if that's with Reed, then so be it. Just don't shut me out," he says and my heart breaks, not just for him, but also for me. No one should ever have to do this. Breaking someone else's heart for the chance to be happy.

My heart and head are screaming at each other, but all I can think about is sand and snow. Is Derek my snow? Am I throwing it all away for nothing?

"No what ifs, Rye," he says and I stare at him with my eyes filled with tears. "If you come back, I won't let you go again. It's ripping me apart to do it now, but I don't want you to ever wonder. I want you to be sure."

I see Derek falling apart right before me and I want to comfort him, but it is me causing him this pain.

"I can't believe…I *still* can't believe…I still want him after all this," I say softly, a part of me hoping Derek will use some logic to help me stay here with him. To be happy with him because I know we could be, even if there is still that chance we could be happier with other people.

"That's why I love you, Rye. You never count someone out until you've done everything you can to make sure there isn't anything worth saving there. You still have some shit to work out, but I'm still going to be your best friend. Nothing anyone can say will change that."

I hug him tightly knowing this is what has to be done. A part of me knows how much this man must love me, if he's letting me go to make me happy. My heart twists because I know if I'm happy, he will be miserable. Silently I pray that he will find his what if. That girl he has to put it all on the line for.

"You think too highly of me Derek," I whisper against him and he holds me tighter.

"It doesn't matter who you end up with. None of us deserve you. You love without limits and that's why I'm letting you go. Because I need to know if you come back it's because you want to, not because you're scared to see what might come of you and him," he says and I can feel the agony in his voice. "If he ever mistreats you again though it's over. I won't let you be treated any less then you deserve. And Rye, you deserve the world."

Standing in his arms I know I could just stay. My mind wanders to the possibilities of this relationship and then I feel his head lay against the top of mine and all thoughts leave me. I try to live in the moment. No more what ifs.

CHAPTER TWELVE

Imagine we tried…

Jumping into the car, I don't think of anything else but getting to Houston. I can't fathom what is going through either of their minds, but I have to do this my way. Putting my phone on the dash I put it on speakerphone and wait for the ring.

"Riley? Where are you?" Danni asks and I feel like she already knows everything.

"He called?" I ask, even though I don't have to wait for her response to know.

"Riles, he's a mess. He left after the fight with Derek. Reed couldn't handle it. He saw you slipping through his fingers and ran. It's what he does. I am so sorry," she says and I can tell she's trying not to cry on the other end of the call.

"I will come to you as soon as I can. Where are you?" she asks.

"I'm in Derek's car rental," I say and she just sighs into the phone.

"I wish you had told me about Derek. I knew but you never opened up, so I left it alone. I figured if it was something serious you'd tell me when you were ready,"

"It *was* serious, that's why I hid it. I knew on some level that it would hurt the people around us. Then I left for the summer and I just couldn't keep it going. Derek visited, and it was amazing, but, I can't keep trying to imagine possibilities with Reed. I need to know." I leave it at that and wait.

"Wait…where is Derek?" Danni's voice pitch changes and I know she's putting it all together.

"At the airport." I say and I hear her scream in the background.

"Where are you, Riles?" she finally says when she calms down.

"On my way to Houston."

She begins screaming again and I know she's jumping up and down without actually having to see her. "Why are you going to Houston?" she asks hopefully, and I give it to her.

"I'm chasing after your idiot brother who's decided to not let me decide who I love. He's running and I'm chasing after him. So you better tell me what his dorm number is so I don't look like an idiot knocking on every door searching for Reed Humphrey,"

I say quickly and she squeals excitedly (again) into the phone.

"He's an idiot, you're right. But I am so happy to hear you are actually chasing his ass down," Danni exclaims into the phone.

"No more imagining, Danni."

I can hear her crying on the other end of the line and I have to fight hard to keep my eyes clear so I end up in Houston in one piece.

"I love you Riley Dunham, no matter what happens," she says into the phone and I just keep my eyes on the road, trying to keep my emotions in check.

"I love you Daniela Humphrey, no matter what dumbass crap your brother puts me through."

We both laugh, giddy in our own ways and end the call.

Just an hour later, I am pulling up to his building and I look around trying to understand the text directions that Danni sent me. After I get out of the car and make my way to his dorm, a guy in a football jersey is on his way out and holds the door for me. "Someone waiting for you inside or just here to party?" he asks and I forget its Valentine's Day for a moment.

"I'm here for someone," I say with a smile on my face.

"Lucky Bastard," he says, laughing as he walks away.

Standing in front of the door I go to knock and change my mind. "What am I doing here? He ran away from me," I say to myself, turning around and chickening out. The door pulls open and there is Reed with his keys in his hand staring at me like he's seen a ghost.

"Riles," he says, stepping towards me but stops when he sees me take a step back. "I was just coming to get you," he says and I want to yell at him but I know that's not why I came here.

"I love you," I blurt out and my eyes pop open. That was not what I was planning to say but it comes out anyway.

Reed grabs me and pulls me into his room shutting the door and pushing me against it at the same time. "Why did you come, Riles?"

"I called Danni and got your information," I say.

He shakes his head at me. "Not how. Why," he demands and I bring my hand up to the side of his face as he leans into me.

"Because I love this guy who has a thing about running away, so I had no choice but to chase after him. But, fair warning. I'm done chasing. Either love me back or let me go…forever," I say boldly.

CHAPTER THIRTEEN

Imagine I believed…

It's been two weeks since that day I knocked on the door at Reed's. Two weeks of him constantly calling me and visiting when he didn't have class. Standing in the airport with him, I feel anxious. His sister and family are finally coming out for a new cruise. We haven't told them. I'm not sure if he's hiding it or if it just didn't come up. Danni knows because she's called me a hundred times asking everything except if we've done it.

Which we haven't, I want to be sure. There are certain things that can't be taken back and losing my virginity is one of them. I love him and he knows that. That's all that matters to either of us.

Derek has stuck by his word. He hasn't asked me about what happened, he just continues to be my best friend, calling me and talking about courses, summer plans, but never about my relationship. It's nice and normal. Exactly what we need in our 'strictly friends' friendship. Reed knows about Derek and me, there are no secrets between us now and he has accepted it. When I told him what Derek did for me, he was surprised, but he said he was willing to do the same thing.

Living a life without trying to imagine every outcome has been exactly what I needed. My decision was the right one. Does that mean it's all rainbows and sunshine? Probably not, but whatever happens we are in it together and that's a first for Reed and me, after all these years.

Reed squeezes my hand, pulling me from my internal thoughts and nods forward. I see his family coming through and I let go of his hand, taking a tiny step away from him.

Reed's eyes flash to me and I turn slightly so I don't have to look at him and make this anymore awkward.

"What the fuck, Riles?" he says putting his hand out for me to grab it.

I stare down at it, shaking my head instead of grabbing it. "They don't know about us—you didn't tell them. I know because Danni has been keeping it a secret until you tell them," I say with a bit of hurt in my voice.

He grabs my hand, pulls me to him and kisses me intensely, all while never letting go of my hand. He pulls away with a chuckle and I glare at him. "There is no question now is there? Riley, I would never keep you a secret. I love you and my family already loves you."

As I turn, I see his mom and dad staring at us, pleasantly shocked, and Danni is excitedly clapping her hands together. It's their mom who moves first running up to us, hugging us tightly together. When she pulls away I see tears in her eyes and I fight to hold myself together. She is a mess and can't say anything.

Danni runs over, hugging me tightly after her mom lets us go. Turning to her brother she glares at him. "You're an idiot. If you hurt her, I will disown you and adopt her. Got it?"

Reed puts his hand up in a defensive gesture while laughing. "Yeah, easy Danni, we are in an airport. I'd hate for you to get arrested and miss this vacation. Actually, I wouldn't. Help, someone help me," he teases and she smacks him. "Hey, if it gets me more time without having to share my girl, I will do whatever I have to," he says and I lean into him, hugging him tightly.

His dad walks up and shakes hands with Reed, winking at him. Then he moves on to me, hugging me in a big bear hug. "It's been too quiet around my house without my girls."

Suddenly I'm pulled away and Reed wraps his arms around me. "My girl, dad, but you can keep the other one," he says with a grin and I elbow him softly in the stomach, causing his dad to laugh. Reed leans down and kisses me softly before turning his attention back to his family.

His mom looks like she's ready to burst and she claps her hands together laughing and crying at the same time. "Finally," she says.

Yes, Finally.

Copyright © 2018 by Gracie Wilson.

Other books in the series:

- BEAUTIFULLY DESTROYED
- BEAUTIFULLY FORGOTTEN

Our columnist, Julie Pitzel, has been a receptionist, radio DJ, bill collector, telemarketer, administrative assistant, community college instructor, and an expediter (aka professional nag). She's been involved in the Houston writing community for many years including two years as President of a local Romance Writers of America Chapter. She writes paranormal fiction from a geodesic dome south of Houston, where she lives with her husband and a pair of cats. Most recently, her story "The Dance" was published in The Death of All Things" *anthology.*

WEDDING NIGHT

by Julie Pitzel

(Soft music ~ sweet perfume)
Champagne chilling by the bed

(Candle light ~ two alone)
Loving words coyly said

(A kiss ~ caress)
"Do Not Disturb" on the door

(A bit of lace ~ piece of silk)
Clothing dropped upon the floor

(Gentle embrace ~ nervous laugh)
Covers turned on the bed

(Twisted sheet ~ tangled feet)
On the night you are wed

Copyright © 2018 by Julie Pitzel.

YOU READ THAT?: EVOLUTION OF THE HERO

by Julie Pitzel

When people mention romance heroes, most of us think of pirates, CEOs, princes, and men-in-uniform. Bad-boys, leaders, the dominant men who must direct the action. In short, we think of alpha males.

So many of our traditional romance heroes fit the alpha description; they tend to be commanding and decisive. They have instinctive control of the world around them, and they don't give up power easily. We love watching them lose that control when the heroine enters their life, disrupting their plans and processes.

But not all alpha males are heroes. There's a fine line between taking charge and dictating, between being dominant and bullying, between steadfast and inflexible. And while many of us enjoy watching or reading about macho men doing manly things, we don't want them following us home. Too many of us have experience with real-life alphas, and prefer keeping them out of our escape fiction.

Enter the beta hero. I'm not sure when they were first introduced, but I do remember discussions and debates wondering who would want to read about these "wimpy" heroes. They were perfectly fine as secondary characters, maybe okay for low-action family dramas, or wallflower-in-reverse stories. But they didn't quite meet the heartthrob quotient.

Beta males are often described as indecisive, weaklings, followers who let women take charge. A beta hero was apt to be a school teacher or scientist. A man who spent too much time thinking and not enough time doing (horrors!). Betas were considered…nice, which equates to somewhat bland. How long would romance readers put up with nice, boring heroes?

This was the state of the romance hero at least through the beginning of the twenty-first century. On one hand there were alphas: fun and exciting heroes, who could make a girl orgasm with a look but didn't know how to pick up their own socks. And betas on the other: a great helpmate, who would change diapers without complaint, but couldn't find a g-spot with a map.

At least that was the perception.

I believe gothic romances gave rise to the alpha hero and fostered their less appealing characteristics. These dark, brooding, distant heroes professed love for the heroine, married her, and whisked her off to a remote castle. As soon as the couple settled in, he'd get cold and secretive. When someone attempted to harm or scare the heroine, he'd often question her observations, effectively gas-lighting her.

Most gothics and early romances were told from the heroine's point of view, which made it difficult to understand or empathize with the hero. These men frequently came off as jerks and were easily suspected of being the villains. Then, our hero would swoop in at the last minute and save the heroine from the actual villain, revealing that had been his plan all along. We didn't get to experience the hero's thoughts and feelings; we didn't know his motivations until he explained them after saving the day.

When the romance industry blew up in the eighties, it became common to switch points of view. We finally got to see part of the story through the hero's eyes. They still retained some of their gothic roots—brooding and secretive, but they had progressed a little. They were more complex and the reader knew their goals and motivations. Even if we still thought they were acting like rat bastards, we at least knew why.

I'm not really sure why beta heroes got such a bad reputation. They may not have the tough persona of an alpha, but they were still effective heroes. Yes, they frequently starred in family dramas or sweet romances—stories centered around moral dilemmas where no one is physically threatened. But they would step up and take on the emotional risk, which is itself very sexy. When a beta was the lead in a romantic suspense or action adventure, they may have been reluctant, but they ultimately faced the challenge. And beta heroes were more than sufficient in the bedroom. They might not take the heroine against a wall, but bedroom gymnastics aren't for everyone.

The main difference seemed to be that a beta hero was more often willing to work with the heroine. They weren't afraid to admit that they didn't have the answers, that they weren't sure of the next step. They were willing to take input, whereas the alpha hero frequently had to be pushed to accept help or direction by the heroine, or anyone they consider under their protection.

Long before #MeToo, the romance industry was drifting away from the strict archetypes. We may have been ahead of the curve on this issue. According to *The Myth of the Alpha Male,* during a study in 1987, women preferred the dominant rather than submissive men. At least that's what they wanted for sexual partners, but maybe not so much for marital partners. In 1999, when they revisited the study, they realized it was missing a control—scenarios with neither dominant nor submissive traits displayed. The test subjects initially preferred the men in the control. Adjusting the study after the initial results, they figured out that the partners women found the sexiest—and also wanted to marry—were confident, easygoing, assertive, and sensitive, an even combination of dominant and non-dominant traits—a mixture of alphas and betas. The romance industry didn't need this study. Our writers were already turning out more balanced heroes.

The lines kept crossing. Now it's a little more challenging to tell the difference between an alpha and a beta hero in most of our stories. Fewer of our protagonists fit in those preconceived boxes. A mostly alpha hero may display complex emotions and request advice from the heroine. A mostly beta hero may lead the mission even though it takes him out of his comfort zone. It's become difficult to classify our heroes as strictly alpha or beta, unless we're dealing with werewolves.

If we were to compare today's heroes with the heroes created in the eighties, many of today's would be considered betas. They aren't indecisive or weak, but they listen to the heroine. They're more apt to display emotion. They're more apt to think and plan instead of simply doing. Turns out romance readers *did* like the beta heroes and some of those traits got absorbed by the alphas. One of the biggest changes is the rise of explicit consent. The alphas of old didn't wait for permission.

As the romance industry progressed, so did our heroes. It was somewhat inevitable because our heroines are evolving. The women at the center of these stories are often the CEOs and pirates and starship captains. They are not waiting to be rescued. They aren't wringing their hands and hoping for a white knight. Today's heroine is going to put on her big-girl panties and accept the challenges thrown at her. In some cases, she's also going to pull on the thigh-high boots and grab a whip because that's what she needs to solve the problem.

Today's romance heroines are taking the initiative to overcome their own difficulties. They may ask for help from the hero, but they aren't dependent on him. They are fighting their own fights and saving themselves from the railroad tracks. And sometimes saving the hero as well.

Our heroines are no longer looking for heroes, they're looking for partners. The heroes had to evolve.

Copyright © 2018 by Julie Pitzel.

Reference:

https://www.artofmanliness.com/articles/ the-myth-of-the-alpha-male/

Karen McCoy writes YA and middle grade fantasy and science fiction. Outside her librarian career, she's contributed to reviews for Library Journal *and* Children's Literature. *In January 2012, she sold a feature article to* School Library Journal *entitled, "What Teens are Really Reading," and contributed a chapter to* Now Write! Science Fiction, Fantasy, and Horror, *published in February 2014 from Penguin Random House. She has experience as a book buyer for teen and children's books, and maintains a blog,* The Writer Librarian, *where she interviews at least one author a week. For more information, or to subscribe to her newsletter, you can visit www.karenmccoy.net.*

HOW DIFFERENT VOICES ARE CHANGING THE YA ROMANCE LANDSCAPE

by Karen McCoy

Romance tropes. As readers, we have a love/hate relationship with them. The love triangle. The Cyrano. Instantaneous love at first sight. While these are often still found in books, the literature is breaking these molds and moving in newer directions. One onus that is driving this is a more widely diverse set of protagonists, especially with the continued Own Voices movement. We are seeing more diverse protagonists in adult romance stories—as evidenced by *The Kiss Quotient* by Helen Hoang, where Stella, our main female protagonist, is on the autism spectrum.

Similar strides are being made in YA, with characters mirroring the variety of diversity we'd see in real life—and giving readers a chance to embrace a wider selection of stories they can identify with. Here are a few different varietals of protagonist that people might consider adding to their to-be-read lists:

The Left-Brained Protagonist

YA protagonists are emerging in all different stripes. They can often be from different cultural backgrounds, as well as gender and sexual identities, which often takes stories beyond the typical "not like other girls" and "not like other boys" parameters,

which, when left unchecked can create a problematic narrative. And, when overdone, "not like other girls/boys" often hammers in the message that femininity is undesirable. Plots now are exploring and pushing against that boundary, allowing for various character traits to be acceptable in both our young men and young women. Breaking damaging stereotypes is one way Own Voices has strengthened the industry. Newer protagonists, particularly heroines, are more often foraying into STEM (Science, Technology, Engineering, and Mathematics) interests—especially in romance stories.

In *When Dimple Met Rishi* by Sandhya Menon, Dimple is a web developer trying to find her own identity amid her familial and cultural expectations. Dimple doesn't just have an "aversion to make-up and fashion." Her journey demonstrates the barriers women, particularly ethnic women, face when they are in fields of work that are usually dominated by men. The fact that Dimple overcomes this struggle and finds her own truths makes her a heroine to admire. Even more importantly, Rishi loves her as she is—another strong message that likeable protagonists don't necessarily have to fit into the usual parameters.

STEM girls like Dimple are also breaking other stereotypes, like the "Manic Pixie Dream Girl" formula, which is often a problematic trope in YA, forcing a girl "sidekick" to be a mere prop for the male protagonist to help with his character rather than recognizing that she is her own person with needs that are just as important as his. In Gretchen McNeil's *I'm Not Your Manic Pixie Dream Girl*, the protagonist, Bea, comes up with a math formula to figure out why her boyfriend broke up with her—and in doing so, shapes a formula for herself based on the "Manic Pixie Dream Girl" trope. While this isn't technically an Own Voices story, Bea's journey shows how the "Manic Pixie Dream Girl" has made for some pretty two-dimensional heroines. However, part of Bea's overall realization is that she doesn't have to play a role in order to be happy, and that she can live for herself rather than for someone else. In this way, she breaks molds that heroines are often constricted by and given agency.

Overall, the left-brained protagonist shows us what might be possible—especially if we ditch the lies we tell ourselves and societal norms that desirable woman must fit in certain roles and not in others.

The Unwilling Protagonist

Some tropes aren't new, but rather an old classic with a shiny new paint job, such as the case of the unwilling protagonist. Once known as "reluctant heroes," the unwilling protagonist is defined by their hesitation, which often comes from within, rather than being defined by someone else, or some external force.

Perhaps one of the most poignant stories I've read with an unwilling protagonist is *Everything, Everything* by Nicola Yoon. Madeline has been kept inside her whole life due to her medical condition. But when Ollie moves in next door, Maddy is faced with a choice: explore what the outside world and Ollie have to offer or stay within the safety of the cocoon she's always known. Her unwillingness is understandable; in order to expand her life, she has to risk losing it. But the conflict is completely internal and involves hard choices that Maddy has to make for herself. It's only when her love grows for Ollie that Maddy can find a way to live her life on her terms, without anyone else defining who she has to be.

Another example of an unwilling protagonist can be found in *Cinderella Boy* by Kristina Meister, which involves protagonist Declan and his sister Delia. Delia catches Declan trying on her clothes and insists that he come to a party with her as "Layla." Declan welcomes the opportunity, but when he's presented to his crush, Carter, and Carter starts to fall for "Layla," Declan grows a conscience and puts distance between himself and Carter. Usually this kind of distance acts as a foil in a romance story, but in *Cinderella Boy*, the distance ends up redefining the relationship between Carter and Declan in poignant ways—including what Declan might think is possible for himself.

Denial of growing love can also be seen in Adrienne Young's *Sky in the Deep*—where seventeen-year-old Eelyn has to unwillingly follow the shady Fiske in order to return to her family. What gives Eelyn layers as a character is that her toughness doesn't merely derive from what happens to her—

she is independent and resilient because that is her natural, internal inclination. She gets to choose her own destiny, rather than it being decided for her, and her unwillingness becomes an opportunity to adapt. As Eudora Welty famously said, "Time as we know it subjectively is often the chronology that stories and novels follow: it is the continuous thread of revelation."

The Rebel Protagonist

This brings us into our last category, or a subset of the unwilling protagonist—the rebel. Rebels have been seen in romance in many different contexts, but in recent books, more protagonists, especially heroines, are more willing to go against the grain of what they're expected to do—using rebellion as a tool to find the hitherto unacknowledged power within themselves. In addition, they have more freedom to be in relationships that aren't necessarily restricted by the traditional parameters.

This can also be applied to different time periods—as seen in Mackenzi Lee's *The Gentleman's Guide to Vice and Virtue*. The story's driving force is Henry "Monty" Montague, who is basically hungover (perhaps still a bit drunk) on the first page. His life is full of bad decisions—and he wouldn't have it any other way—until it puts him, and the boy he loves, Percy, in danger. In Monty's story, one character does not "fix" or re-define the other. Instead, Monty and Percy can each be what they want—without feeling that they have to change themselves.

The same rebel theme can also be seen in Kami Garcia's 2017 YA romance novel, *The Lovely Reckless*. Garcia is most well-known as a co-author of *Beautiful Creatures*, but *The Lovely Reckless* shows that breaking the rules can help a protagonist find ways to redefine what they believe to be true about themselves. Frankie, a former straight-A student, witnesses the murder of her boyfriend, and her downward spiral ends with a DUI and community service. But when she gets to know the equally troubled Marco Leone, she discovers that being a bit broken doesn't mean you have to break, and that it's possible to redefine yourself into new and unexpected shapes. Therefore, the role of rebel doesn't always have to be solely destructive—instead, it can show characters parts of themselves that they might not otherwise have explored.

There's no doubt that tropes in both YA and other romance stories will continue to adapt, while the old standards remain. It's up to readers to decide which books speak to them. Ultimately, I'm a firm believer that every book on the shelf has its reader—as long as a reader can find it. And if trends like the above continue, more readers are not only going to find themselves in books—authors can find new readers too.

Copyright © 2018 by Karen McCoy.

Read a wonderful article in the *New York Times* about The Kiss Quotient here,

https://www.nytimes.com/2018/07/07/books/romance-novels-diversity.html

C.S. DeAvilla *writes award-winning science fiction, fantasy, and romance under another pen name. She has been a romance fan since she sneaked a peek at her mother's massive historical romance bookcase and fell in love with all the characters. She reads every romance genre—as long as two people are falling in love, she'll give it a read. Her favorite authors are Jennifer Crusie, J.R. Ward, Darynda Jones, Suzanne Brockmann, Sarah MacLean, and Kristan Higgins. But she always has room for one more.*

RECOMMENDED BOOKS

by C.S. DeAvilla

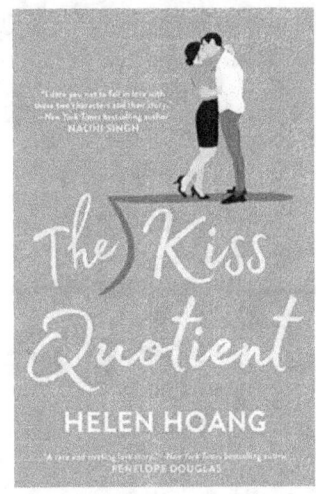

Title: *The Kiss Quotient*
Author: Helen Hoang
Publisher: Berkley
ASIN: B075HXST4P
Release Date: June 5th, 2018

I saw some early reviews of *The Kiss Quotient* stream by on my social media feed and quickly looked up the book. An economics-math geek who decides to take love to a scientific level? I'm in. I was in at the first lines of the description and the cute title with equally adorable cover. However, this is more than just a fun read. Stella, not quite understanding love, is convinced she's missing some hidden puzzle—being on the spectrum makes it even more difficult for her to decide if it's something about her personality or her inexperience that leaves her wishing for more. So, she hires a male escort, Michael Phan, to teach her everything she would possibly need to know about seducing the perfect mate. That plan soon leads to testing out a fake relationship and cue one of the best romantic tropes with a new twist. I adored Stella and Michael. Their story is incredibility compelling and I couldn't put the book down—I needed to know what would happen at their next meeting and their next. This story will melt readers and continue to receive high praise—very deserving of this debut. Helen Hoang is an author to watch.

teammates for the night. However, Rowdy falls for the geeky Scarlett hard and fast, throwing a curveball right into his love life. He comes to depend on their weekly Friday meetings where he continues to block her from entering the baseball house, even after her ban is lifted. Except Rowdy doesn't want to share her. These two characters will have you hugging your e-reader late into the night, fighting for them to finally take the plunge. There is a long lead up to this couple's first kiss, so this is the book for readers who enjoy a slow burn in their romance.

Title: *Jock Row*
Author: Sara Ney
Publisher: Self-Published
ASIN: B07CT6KQB7
Release Date: May 1st, 2018

Sara Ney very quickly jumped into my must-buy list over the last year with her *How to Date a Douchebag* series. I enjoyed how she evolved the series into championing nice guys who finished first. *Jock Row* follows in this same theme. Scarlett is the responsible college student who is that designated friend at the party keeping her friends from doing something they'll regret. She can sniff out a jerk in their midst quicker than a bloodhound, a skill that earns her a ban from the baseball house. Rowdy Wade's job is to make sure she doesn't continue to cockblock his

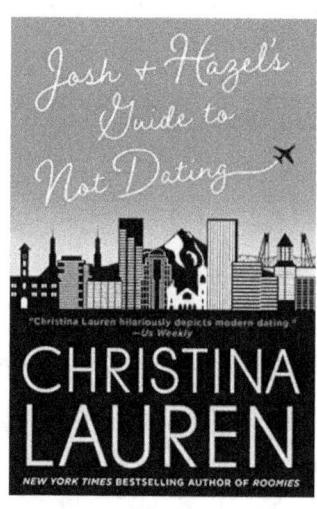

Title: *Josh and Hazel's Guide to Not Dating*
Author: Christina Lauren
Publisher: Galley (Simon & Schuster)
ASIN: B07CL8YSK1
Release Date: Sept 4th, 2018

I've quickly become a die-hard fan of the writing duo who go by the pen name Christina Lauren. They have a fun, easy style that takes the reader into emotionally deep storylines, creating a smart mix of humor hits and fascinating character and relationship profiles. From the first chapter, readers fall for the main character Hazel. She's unconventional, right from the first page when readers are treated to a summary of Hazel's first interactions with the smart and quiet Josh. For one, she declares her desire to sleep with him and then promptly vomits on his shoes, an event that becomes an in-joke between them for years to come, even after they both graduate from college. Hazel never forgets her friendship with Josh, vowing that it could never be anything more after she got to know him. Her fear was that if they dated, they'd never be the same and she'd lose her best friend. Fast forward a few years and Hazel is working as a teacher, newly hired at a fancy private school. Her new best friend's husband is her new boss and guess who shows up at the welcome party hosted at her best friend's house? Josh. And he's her best friend's brother. What? In a coincidence that totally works for the romance set up they quickly fall back into friend-love with each other with the help of a cheating girlfriend (Josh's) and leaky pipes that require a place to stay (Hazel's latest disaster). Josh and Hazel, not accepting their attraction to each other, decide instead to set each other up on a series of dates—each ending in disaster. But what isn't a disaster is the love that slowly builds between these two mis-matched partners and all they have to do is stop "not dating" long enough to realize it. This is another winner from Christina Lauren that current fans will love, and readers who haven't yet discovered the amazingness that awaits will see a lot of similarities between Lauren and Rainbow Rowell, Kristan Higgins, Jennifer Crusie, and other romantic comedy greats.

Title: *Lickety Split*
Author: Damon Suede
Publisher: Dreamspinner Press
ASIN: B06X9H7PGL
Release Date: March 13th, 2017

Patch Hastle isn't thrilled about inheriting his parents' ranch. He hated everything about growing up in Texas where his only memories are how he never measured up to his father's expectations. Worst of all, he'll have to face Tucker Biggs again—his father's best friend who can push every button Patch has, including getting him all hot and bothered. Tucker's goal is to simply get the ranch ready for whatever Patch would like to do—whether that be sell or stay. Patch is certain Tucker has an ulterior motive in mind, he just needs to figure it out. Except it doesn't take long for the two men to fall in love and complicate all of Patch's decisions, because Patch will never stay in Texas and Tucker will never leave. Suede has a rough style that is authentic, genuine, and matches the rugged characters he writes about. Readers who have been looking for a romance between characters who have a large age difference will enjoy *Lickety Split*.

was under a new publisher and with change comes a chance to reinvent and really get to the heart of what makes a series a winner. Ward has done plenty of contemporary romances with success, but this… this is something special. Right out of the gate this series start is blazing. Hot. I have to admit, as a huge fan of the Black Dagger Brotherhood, I didn't think any other series J.R. Ward could write would come close, but this Firefighters series is competing fiercely for that top spot.

Copyright © 2018 by C.S. DeAvilla.

Title: ***Consumed***
Author: J.R. Ward
Publisher: Simon & Schuster
ISBN: 1501194909
Release Date: October 9th 2018

Nothing makes me happier than a new J.R. Ward book. There's a reason she's on auto-buy lists for so many readers. But this review isn't to gush about her latest paranormal release, which are fabulous by the way, but to pick my jaw up off the floor over her newest series opener, *Consumed*. Anne Ashburn's entire identity is wrapped up in being a firefighter, so when her career goes up in flames during a warehouse fire, Danny McGuire decides he can never forgive himself for being the reason she lost it all. Except Anne is a fighter and her new career as a fire investigator keeps her in the action and in Danny's life—much to her annoyance and to his relief. Danny can't stop loving Anne and Anne can't bear to become a kept woman like her mother. The couple has a lot of demons in their respective pasts, but they'll need to confront them if they're going to make it to that oh-so-satisfying HEA. The novel begins right in the action and doesn't let up from that level of intensity—especially the attraction between Anne and Danny. The group of firefighter's friendship-bond interactions were a delightful bonus. Romance books have an edge on relationships of all kinds and that special recipe of "a band of fighters that are closer than family" is what Ward does best—and all her skills are shining in *Consumed*. I noticed that the series

Andrea attended The Culinary Institute of America in Hyde Park, New York to study Culinary Arts in 1998. Upon graduation, she continued on at Johnson & Wales University in Providence, RI to study Food Service Management. After a few years of getting hands-on experience, Andrea was drawn to Chicago to the famed Charlie Trotters Restaurant. There, Andrea was exposed to one-of-a-kind wine cellar in which she received one of the best wine educations in the world, tasting & serving some to the most rare and most special wines ever produced. She worked with some of the world's top ingredients, Chef's, Farmers, food lover's and wine aficionados, but homesick, Andrea returned to Santa Fe, NM, where she was Partner & Head Chef at Rasa Juice Bar & Ayurveda. Andrea received many rave reviews and won the Local Hero Award 2 years in a row for her organic, plant-based café. Her attention to detail to her beautifully plated and delicious food is enhanced with the love and care she enfuses into every bite! She is currently the Owner and Chef of The Temptress Private Chef & Catering operated out of her home town of Santa Fe, NM.

dulge yourself. The next two issues will cover Christmas and Valentine's Day, guaranteeing an inclusion of decadent sweets and seasonal favorites with a twist, so I figured for my first recipe in this magazine, we'd go for something healthy, but also tasty, to help us all fit into our date night's best attire. Enjoy!

MAIN INGREDIENTS

- 2 heads cauliflower
- 3 cups cashews (soaked) for 30 mins
- ½ cup nutritional yeast
- lemon juice—1 lemon
- ½ teaspoon paprika
- ½ teaspoon cayenne or to taste
- 1 tsp salt, taste sauce to adjust
- 1 cup water, add more to adjust consistency

DIRECTIONS

Chop cauliflower to small florets (do not leave stems as they will be tough to cook). Place in large bowl.

Drain water from soaking cashews, add to vitamix.

Add remaining ingredients and blend to a smooth cream.

Season to your preference. Add salt and water to ensure a creamy, tasty sauce.

Toss sauce with chopped cauliflower. Add to crockpot.

THE TEMPTRESS PRESENTS: FAMOUS CAULIFLOWER MAC & CHEESE

Vegan & Gluten Free

by Andrea Abedi

I'm delighted to become a contributor to *Heart's Kiss*, and I'm looking forward to tempting you with delicious dishes that would be perfect for date night with your partner, or just simply to in-

Pour about ½ cup of water to crockpot to ensure that it does not burn. Stir to mix water and cream.

Cook for about 1.5 hours, stirring often so it does not catch.

ALMOND TOPPING

2 cups organic raw almonds

1 cup chopped parsley

1 tablespoon sea salt

Add all ingredients to food processor and mix until all ingredients are chopped finely, but not ground. Add liberally to your dish with love and a flourish.

Copyright © 2018 by Andrea Abedi.

Lezli Robyn is an Australian multi-genre author and Assistant Publisher of Arc Manor, living in the US with her mini-Dachshund/Chihuahua, Bindi. Her love of books led to her meeting her future collaborator, Mike Resnick, on eBay. Since that serendipitous event Lezli has sold to prestigious markets around the world and is in the process of finishing too more small press books while writing her first two novels. Known for her bittersweet and heart-tugging writing technique, she has been a finalist for several prestigious awards, including the 2010 Campbell Award for Best New Writer. In 2011 and 2014 she also won the Catalan Premi Ictineu Award for Best Translated Story. You can find her at www.lezlirobyn.com.

HEART'S KISS' FIRST RENDEZVOUS WITH THE ROMANCE WRITERS OF AMERICA CONFERENCE

by Lezli Robyn

In lieu of a closing editorial this issue, I thought I would share some behind-the-scenes moments of our magazine family with our readers this issue. My co-editor, Tina Smith, our publisher, Shahid Mahmud, and yours truly went to our first RWA conference as the creators of *Heart's Kiss* magazine, and to say we were overwhelmed by the amazing reception we received there is an understatement.

Tina and I had a blast attending the entire conference together, and my boss, Shahid—who admits he doesn't know anything about romance—said he loved attending the Trade Show with us. He noted how much it touched him when attendees would thank us for the free *Heart's Kiss* lipsticks—which readers all thought was wonderfully appropriate advertising—as well as the raffling of e-readers and free subscriptions to the magazine!

When I arrived the day before the conference I was delighted to spend an hour talking to Rita Clay Estrada, the first RWA President, and the amazing author whom the RITA Awards are named after. It was clear this conference was going to be a good one, starting with such a highlight.

Then, the next day, before I attended a three-hour seminar on newsletter tricks of the trade (very insightful) I met up with one of our authors we interviewed for Issue 9 of our magazine, the wonderful Beverly Jenkins! Her kindness and happiness to meet the Aussie behind the emails was the capper for a great first day. Of course, we took a selfie.

Tina, a veteran of RWA conferences, showed me around the events, taking me to my first mass Harlequin signing. On the way, we discovered her novels in the bookshop, being a speaker at this conference. At the signing, we met an author we serialized in issues 7, 8 and 9 of *Heart's Kiss*, Anna J. Stewart (far right of the group photo).

The next day we were delighted to be one of the publishers featured at the Trade Show, where we met even more of our authors and were able to connect with current and future readers of our magazine. You can see we had a wonderful time. The next photo shows fan-favorite author, L. Penelope, standing behind our table. We ran out of copies of our first three issues of the magazine before the event was over! The following photo shows the bustle of activity at our table, where a lot of attendees told us that they had been hearing about our *Heart's Kiss* bags all day from other writers and readers who had taken photos of them, and they wanted to know where they could buy them. I had created the bags for Tina and me as a present for us for the hard work of putting a new magazine together. I had no idea they would be so popular…but more about the bag later!

Tina and I didn't miss any opportunity to pose with the writer family we are creating in our magazine. Our writers have commented on how they really feel we are creating a community they are loving being a part of, and Tina and I couldn't be prouder of the authors we are publishing each issue. Before we leave the Trade Show, I posed with L. Penelope, and then I took a photo of Tina with Susan Donovan, the latter of which we are interviewing and publishing a new, exclusive novella by in our upcoming Christmas issue.

Following the trade show I interviewed the incomparable Brenda Jackson (who was surrounded by a lot of delightful fans when I first met her), for this issue of *Heart's Kiss*. I think you all will agree with me, after reading that interview, how moving it was to talk with this amazing woman and how much I learned about about what it was like to grow up in a country that once considered her a minority. Not only is her life and lifetime love a testament to how much she has conquered the stereotypes that tried but failed to hold her back, but she was also just so incredibly warm and fascinating. Her innate sense of humor struck a cord with my Aussie quirkiness and I'm ecstatic that she will be writing us a new novella for our Valentine's issue!

and then we ran into Leslye again. I took a photo of her with Tina in front of the conference's official banner, because there can never be enough photos.

The next day I attended my co-editor's 20/20 workshop on how to accurately portray service animals in romance fiction. Not only was her knowledge in the field so insightful, but it was wonderful to see that the room was filled with attendees not only staying for her first presentation, but her repeat presentations so they could ask her *more* questions at the end of the next session.

It turns out that inadvertent catch-up led to an even more special meeting. Fans of one of our authors, Alia Mahmud, came up to us, all excited. They had been trying to find us for four days (!!!) to tell us how much Alia's fiction had meant to them, as parents of a Muslim child also of the same name. They thought she was an amazing role model for young women and we could not agree more. We were so moved by their words and only wished Alia could have been with us to hear them for herself.

The rest of Friday was filled with the both of us attending appointments with various editors and publicists of major romance publishers and imprints to create reciprocal relationships between our publishing companies (so we can bring our readers more exclusive interviews, reviews, fiction and articles from the top writers in the field), but Saturday was all about our authors. We had breakfast with Anna J. Stewart and Melinda Curtis (who we failed to capture on film!),

Afterwards we raced over Brenda Novak's event, where her and Debbie Mason interviewed each other about their careers. The room was filled with lots of fans, yummy cupcakes and bags filled with free goodies. Tina and I are thrilled to have published a short story of Brenda's in *Heart's Kiss* and look forward to interviewing her in a future issue. Here are some photos from the event, to show you how well received it was! (I promise you Brenda and I didn't consult each other on what we were going to wear!)

Our last event of the day, and our last action of the conference as co-editors of *Heart's Kiss*, was a wonderful dinner at a scrumptious Italian restaurant with myself, L. Penelope (both of us not pictured below), Tina, her husband, Tyler Smith, our columnist, Julie Pitzel, and hidden behind her, her husband, Bob Mann, and the featured author of our upcoming Christmas issue, Susan Donovan. We could not wish for better authors for our magazine; the dinner was a wonderful end for a wonderful conference.

Thank you for putting your faith in us, and please keep supporting us by buying our issues for yourself and your family and friends. If the buzz at the conference is anything to go by, we could really make a big hit out of this magazine, but it will only happen with the help of our readers. We are looking forward to continuing this journey with you!

Photos and article copyright © 2018
by Lezli Robyn.

We would love to thank the members of RWA for accepting us so warmly in Denver; we loved getting to meet our writers in person and experience the warm ambience that is the annual Romance Writers of America conference. We'll leave you with this little teaser…

Remember how I said I would get back to that bag again? Well, last but not least, here is a photo of the bag I created (with the gorgeous cover image from issue 10) and the books of authors Tina and I met at the conference who *all* agreed to provide content for future issues of our magazine! I think you can agree, from the names you see on the top of those book stacks, that we will have some amazing content for our readers in the upcoming year.